Susan lu

Without thinking about what she was doing, Susan swept the dagger from the floor. Seizing it by the blade, she held it out in front of her.

"Go!" she cried. She lunged forward and thrust the dagger into Bishop's face.

There was a flash of blue fire, and then Bishop's agonized scream filled the room with a horrible sound. He fell backward against a chair, knocking it to the floor with a crash. His flesh was seared where the cross had touched his cheek. Then he launched himself forward in a writhing, twisting dive through the window. In the darkness outside, Susan could see a sudden flash; then there was nothing but a dying scream.

Susan shut her eyes. When she opened them, she saw the dagger in her hands pulsing with a powerful blue light.

Read these terrifying thrillers
from HarperPaperbacks!

Baby-sitter's Nightmare
Sweet Dreams
Sweetheart
Teen Idol
Running Scared
by Kate Daniel

And don't miss M. C. Sumner's
horrifying new trilogy

The Principal
The Substitute *
The Coach *

* coming soon

VAMPIRE'S KISS

Nicholas Adams

HarperPaperbacks
A Division of HarperCollins*Publishers*

This is a work of fiction. The characters, incidents, and
dialogues are products of the author's imagination and are not
to be construed as real. Any resemblance to actual events or per-
sons, living or dead, is entirely coincidental.

HarperPaperbacks   A Division of HarperCollinsPublishers
                   10 East 53rd Street, New York, N.Y. 10022

Copyright © 1994 by Susan Albert

Cover art copyright © 1994 Daniel Weiss Associates, Inc.

All rights reserved. No part of this book may be used or repro-
duced in any manner whatsoever without written
permission of the publisher, except in the case of brief
quotations embodied in critical articles and reviews. For infor-
mation address Daniel Weiss Associates, Inc., 33 West 17th
Street, New York, New York 10011.

Produced by Daniel Weiss Associates, Inc., 33 West 17th Street,
New York, New York 10011.

First printing: March, 1994

Printed in the United States of America

HarperPaperbacks and colophon are trademarks of
HarperCollinsPublishers

10 9 8 7 6 5 4 3 2 1

For Susan and Bill Albert—
thanks for all your help.

VAMPIRE'S KISS

One

![divider]

"We'll be back in a moment with our wrap-up story for this Tuesday night. This is KGTX-TV, Channel Five, Galveston, Texas. Stay with us." The pretty blond anchorwoman smiled into the television camera as a commercial came on.

Susan Scott frowned as she got off the sofa and went into the kitchen. She'd meant to turn on the television at ten to catch the local news, but she'd been so busy moving furniture and hanging curtains in her new apartment that she'd forgotten. Now it was almost ten thirty, and she'd missed most of the report. Oh well. It was summer in Galveston, and nothing much was going on.

Susan opened the refrigerator and took out a soft drink. Her frown changed to a smile as she sat down at the small table where she would eat most of her meals. She pushed her long brown hair out of her eyes and tried to stuff it back into her bandanna. Sure, the kitchen was small, with barely enough room to turn around between the sink and the refrigerator, but the room's size made it efficient—there was only a step between the stove and the refrigerator—and the yellow-checked curtains and framed sunflower print over the table gave it a cheerful sunshiny glow, even at night.

Carrying her drink, Susan went back into the other room. This one was just as cozy as the kitchen. There was the sofa bed, one of those foldaway things, that she'd bought at a flea market. Her sister-in-law had given her the battered coffee table. Her friend Angela had found the pole lamp and the stuffed chair with the saggy cushion at a garage sale. Susan had already covered the back of the sofa with a pretty pink-and-white quilt, and the coffee table would look fine once she refinished it; a little extra stuffing would do wonders for the chair cushion.

Susan sat down on the sofa and leaned back with a tired, happy sigh. She knew she was going to have to devote most of her off-work hours for the next couple of weeks to cleaning and painting, but it was all hers, and that made the wonderful difference.

Not that living with her brother Mack, his wife

Betty, and their two kids, Pete and Randy, had been bad. She really was grateful that they'd been willing and able to give her a home after her parents had been killed in a car accident during her freshman year of high school. Now Susan was seventeen, a grown up, and living alone meant that she was able to take care of herself.

The phone rang and she picked it up. "Hi," Mack said. "Everything okay out there?"

Susan grinned. Mack was a cop and took his vow to serve and protect rather seriously, especially when it came to his kid sister. "Are you checking up on me all the way from El Paso?" she asked.

Mack chuckled. "You bet. Just because I'm on vacation from the force doesn't mean I can't still take care of you, you know. I'm still your big brother, and you're not too big for me to check up on. Even if you have moved out."

"I haven't moved very far," Susan reminded him. "I'm right here over your garage."

"Well, I just wanted to make sure you were settling in okay," Mack said. "Betty and the boys send hugs, and me too. Lock up before you go to bed. Okay?"

"Sure. Thanks, Mack," Susan said. "Good night."

"Good night, Susan. We'll see you in a couple of days."

3

She was smiling when she put down the phone. She was happiest when she was on top of things and in control. And at that moment she was *very* happy. Everything in her life seemed to be falling into place exactly the way she'd planned.

"And now," the anchorwoman announced brightly, "we take you live to a late-breaking story."

Susan turned back to the television. As she did, the screen flickered and the lights in the apartment dimmed momentarily. Susan frowned. When Mack got back, she'd ask him to show her where the circuit breakers were. She probably ought to lay in a supply of candles, too. Now that she was on her own, it was a good idea to prepare for emergencies. Like blackouts and hurricanes.

The lights were burning brightly again, and she was relieved she wouldn't have to worry about the circuit breaker tonight. Or the weather. The TV meteorologist had predicted warm, sunny weather for the next few days. The tourists would love it. They'd ride their rented pedal-powered surreys up and down the busy sidewalks and crowd the beaches with their beach umbrellas and line up by the hundreds to ride the water slide and the bumper cars at Stewart Beach.

Not all the beaches were crowded, though. On the television the scene had shifted to a deserted, windswept stretch of sand. Susan thought how odd that was, considering how beautiful the day had been. A reporter in a jacket and tie stood somberly in the glare of the TV lights. His pale gray-green eyes narrowed as he looked straight into the camera. Behind him, Susan could make out the glimmer of waves and hear the wind in the microphone.

"This is Drew Morris, live from the southeastern end of Galveston Island." The reporter turned slightly and gestured at a group of uniformed men digging into the sand under the glare of floodlights. "We're just off East Beach Drive, behind the SeaWall Condominiums. Earlier this evening two local residents found a shallow grave on the beach here. A few minutes ago police uncovered a body."

Susan stared at Drew Morris's face. The reporter must be new—she couldn't remember seeing him before. And she would *definitely* have remembered him, she told herself. He was dark-haired and good-looking, and he had a deeply resonant voice. It was a description that could fit a half-dozen TV journalists, Susan thought. She leaned forward. What made Drew Morris different was his eyes. There was nothing casual about those eyes. They were probing, powerfully intent—perhaps even a little sad, Susan thought, as if the story he was reporting had some sort of personal significance for him. He turned back to face the camera, and those eyes seemed to fix on hers, to demand her attention.

"The body," he said, "was that of a young man."

Susan shivered a little and turned away from the TV. East Beach Drive? That was only a little way from the motel where her friend Frederica Gardner lived with her mother. Freddie always jogged on the beach at night, that is, when she wasn't singing with one of the local rock groups. Because Freddie had recently auditioned for a new job, she wasn't singing this week. She was probably out there now. She'd be sure to see the cops and the TV cameras. Maybe she was watching Drew Morris doing his live spot right this minute. Susan wondered if his eyes were as deep and mysterious in real life as they were on TV.

The reporter spoke again. "The police haven't yet released the man's identity or the cause of death," he said. There was a tone of deep sadness in his voice. "However, a police spokeswoman said that there were no obvious signs of foul play. But I find this whole case rather suspicious."

Susan couldn't turn away from the screen. Those eyes, those pale gray-green eyes, were fixed on hers with a commanding authority. She sucked in her breath, unaccountably sure that he was speaking directly to *her*. The skin on her arms prickled up into little goose bumps. Of course, that was a silly idea—he was just talking to the camera, the way TV journalists always did. Still, she couldn't

6

escape the conviction that his message was aimed at her, and her alone.

"There are many unknowns in this bizarre case," Drew Morris was saying. "Why would someone bury a young man's body on this windswept beach? Was that person hoping that the secret in this grave would be safe for all eternity?"

He paused for the space of a breath, and then went on, more slowly. "What kind of person would commit another human being to an unmarked grave? And why? These are important questions that demand to be answered." His eyes, steady and unwavering, bored into Susan's, as if he could really see her, as if he could see *through* her. His voice was urgent, pleading. "Please, join me tomorrow night for further details. Maybe together we can solve this mystery."

Another commercial came on. Susan leaned forward and shut the set off. Drew Morris, whoever he was, certainly had a talent for dramatization. It wasn't completely unheard of to find a body on Galveston beach. It didn't happen every day, but careless people sometimes fell off the jetty or off a party boat, and it certainly wouldn't take much of a storm to drift beach sand over a drowning victim. In fact, there had been a storm last week. It could have happened then.

But this new reporter had made this gruesome discovery seem like the strangest, most important thing that had ever happened in Galveston. What's more, he'd made it seem important to *Susan*, as if she were the only person in his audience. He had ordered *her* to listen to his follow-up tomorrow night, as if only she could help him make sense of it all.

Susan stood up and started for the kitchen. She felt chilly, and she shivered. She'd warm herself up with a cup of hot chocolate before she went to bed. Then she stopped. Hot chocolate? In June? That was silly.

Drew Morris had certainly made his point with her. She'd tune in tomorrow night. But whether it was to learn more about the mysterious grave on the beach or to see Drew Morris again, she couldn't be sure. There was one thing she was sure of, she decided, as she checked the lock on the back door and shut off the kitchen light. Drew Morris had the most compelling eyes she had ever seen. Eyes that seemed to look right through her. Eyes that held some deep and impenetrable sadness.

She saw those eyes again that night.

She saw those eyes in her dreams.

Two

Frederica Gardner—Freddie to her friends—thrust her pencil into her curly, copper-red hair, tied her ruffled red-and-white apron around her waist, and touched up her eyeshadow with her little finger. It was Wednesday morning, and her eight-hour shift at the Pizzeria was about to begin. Freddie let out an explosive sigh and shook her head, making a face at the mirror that hung on the wall in the small storage room behind the kitchen. Eleven to nine, with two hours off in the middle of the afternoon. What a drag. Pushing pizzas for the better part of the day. It was too bad that somebody hadn't invented a way you could make honest money without working. There wasn't much to look forward to on her shift except flirting with a few cute customers, like that cool-looking new guy with the dark glasses and the slow, moody smile who'd been in twice last week.

She grinned at the green-eyed girl in the mirror, her copper hair like a curly halo around her freckled face. Yeah. If she could make a living doing vocals with Lenny's rock group, that would almost be like not working. Singing was fun. She considered, sobering a little. No, singing was more than fun. Singing was her life. When she sang, she poured all her feelings, her entire soul, into her music. As far as Freddie was concerned, all music was soul music.

"Hey, Freddie," Angela Sanchez said, coming into the storage room. She hung up her sweater and began twisting her long black hair into a knot at the back of her neck, securing it with a comb.

Angela always looked super with her hair done up that way, Freddie thought with a stab of envy. She shoved a stubborn red curl behind her ear. It didn't hurt that Angie had a great body, either. She wore clothes that hid it, but when you had a figure like that, it was hard to keep it a secret.

"Did you hear from Lenny last night?" Angie asked.

Freddie couldn't help smiling back, even though it wasn't a subject she particularly wanted to talk about. Angie was one of those rare people who make the day seem sunnier just by being there. Maybe it was because she always managed to look on the bright side of things, or because she somehow understood what was on your mind before you unloaded it.

Still, Freddie wasn't sure there was a bright side where Lenny was concerned, and her smile faded. "No, I haven't heard from him yet. What a jerk. I'm beginning to think he's not even going to call. He's probably going to pick that other girl—the one who doubles on guitar." *And who worships the ground he walks on*, she added silently to herself.

She had to admit it, she hadn't knocked them dead at the audition. She frowned at herself in the mirror. She'd looked good, and she'd picked her very strongest songs, the ones she practiced at home with a tape, but when the big moment arrived, she'd been thrown by the band's tempo. And by Lenny's ego. She'd flubbed the first number big time, and things sort of fell apart after that. She'd blown it. She hadn't heard from Lenny since.

Angie turned and put her arms around Freddie. "Hey, listen," she said softly, "don't worry so much about it, okay? I'm sure things will turn out. Maybe Lenny and his band aren't right for you. Maybe that's why the audition didn't go the way you wanted."

"You mean, like we weren't in sync or something?"

11

Angie nodded. "It's very important for people to fit together. Brad says bands can't make good music if they aren't on the same wavelength. If they don't have the same style, the same ideas. I guess musicians are sensitive to stuff like that."

"Yeah, maybe," Freddie said slowly. She wasn't exactly sure what made Brad—Angie's new boyfriend—an authority on harmony. He didn't strike Freddie as being terribly in tune to Angie and her feelings.

But in this case, Freddie told herself, the theory clicked. Lenny was such a jerk, she probably wouldn't ever have gotten in harmony with him, at least not in the way *he'd* want her to. It made her feel better to think that it wasn't lack of talent that had made her bomb the audition. Or her appearance. She gave herself another critical look in the mirror. She didn't exactly look like a rock star. Stupid red hair and a hard, athletic look earned on the tennis court and the track. Not exactly a sex symbol. Unfortunately, that was what Lenny was looking for. Sexy and older. Maybe she should hide out for a year.

"The more I think about it, the more I think you may be right. I didn't fit with Lenny's group," she asserted, leaning against the wall and watching while Angie put on her apron. "They're a pretty tough bunch of guys. If it came right down to it, I'm not sure I'd like to sing in some of the joints

12

where they play. Or wear the kind of clothes they wear." *Or have to stay with them in a darkened basement late at night for rehearsal.* She looked questioningly at Angie. "Know what I mean?"

Angie nodded. "I know." She laughed and straightened her collar. "It's too bad Susan and I don't have your talent for music, Freddie. The three of us would make a great group. *We're* in tune. And we all have the same great fashion sense." Angie dramatically modeled her checked apron as she runway-walked across the room.

"In tune with what?" Susan Scott asked, coming through the door and narrowly missing Angie's kick and turn. Susan was already wearing her apron, and her long brown hair was weaved into a French braid that made her look older than she was. She glanced at her watch. "You certainly don't mean in tune with the clock. If we don't start loading that salad table, we're all in deep trouble."

Freddie grinned. "If we put a group together," she told Angie, "I vote for Susan for drummer."

"Drummer?" Angie asked.

"Yeah," Susan said. "Why the drummer?" She climbed up on a step stool and took a package of napkins off a shelf.

"Because she's got a good sense of timing," Freddie told them. "She keeps us moving." With a giggle she ducked the package of paper napkins Susan tossed at her.

13

"You better believe it," Susan said. "If I didn't keep you moving, who would? You two are so laid-back, you'd be fired tomorrow." Susan thought for a moment. "No. Make that yesterday."

Freddie grinned and picked up the napkins. "You're right," she conceded. "Laid-back and loving it."

"Come on," Angie said, putting her arms around both of them. "Time for the salad squad. Spinach, here we come."

Laughing, the three girls went into the kitchen, where a couple of other people were already at work mixing pizza dough. Susan opened the walk-in cooler and pulled out bowls of chopped veggies. The girls began to load the bowls onto a cart for the salad bar.

A few minutes later, Susan paused beside Freddie. "Did you run on the beach last night, Freddie?"

Freddie added a bowl of cold pasta to the cart. "Yeah, sure." In her otherwise haphazard life, running was the most disciplined thing she did. It helped her keep her weight down—weight could be a problem, working at the Pizzeria. Whoever saw a fat rock star? Opera and jazz, maybe, but not rock.

"I went out about nine thirty," she added. "I got back in time for the late show."

Susan pushed the cart into the dining room

14

where Angela was stacking plates at one end of the salad bar. "Then you must have seen the police digging on the beach behind the SeaWall Condos. Did you stop for a look?"

Freddie started unloading the cart, helping herself to a small pickle. "Police? Digging? I didn't see any digging."

Susan paused and turned. "You didn't see a bunch of cops and a TV crew? Off East Beach Drive?"

Freddie shook her red curls emphatically. "Nope. No cops, no crew." She put down a bowl of radishes, sticking a couple in her pocket. She couldn't get fat on radishes if she tried. "I'm pretty sure I would have noticed something like that," she added. "The beach was totally deserted all the way up to Apffel Park. Three miles of me and the moon and a few drowsy gulls. My favorite kind of night."

Susan stared at her. "No TV crew? But he *said*—" She stopped, looking puzzled. "Are you sure?"

Freddie frowned. "Susan, believe me. There was no TV crew. Unless they were shooting with hidden cameras. You know, like they were buried in the sand or something. Or maybe they were shooting with a periscope! Or hiding in the dunes, disguised as beach grass. Or maybe a creature from—"

Susan smiled. "Okay, okay. I guess I made a mistake," she said slowly. "But I could have sworn—"

"No swearing on the job," Angie said with a laugh.

"Right," Freddie said. "Maybe you just need a good night's sleep." She turned away to push the empty cart back into the kitchen, so she couldn't see the look of fear that had come into Susan's usually calm hazel eyes.

Three

Angela Sanchez put one pizza down in front of her aunt Carlota and handed the other to her younger sister Juanita. She liked it when her family came into the Pizzeria to eat. Nita was her favorite sister, and Aunt Carlota, who lived next door to Angie, was her favorite aunt. In fact, the three of them looked a great deal alike, with long black hair and big brown eyes.

"Would you two like to come over tonight?" Aunt Carlota asked. She leaned forward with a conspiratorial smile. "Don't tell your father, but I'm having a few friends over for an evening of fortune-telling. Maybe you'd like to have a glimpse into your futures, no?"

Angie laughed. "Are you kidding? I wouldn't

17

tell Dad that—not if I wanted to come, anyway."
Her father accused Aunt Carlota, who was Angie's
mother's sister, of being a witch. Actually, Aunt
Carlota saw herself as a *curandera*, a woman who
practices white magic. She was able to use the tra-
ditional healing herbs, potions, and amulets that
had been a way of life in Old Mexico. Friends and
family came to Aunt Carlota for all kinds of mysti-
cal and magical help—from casting spells to healing illnesses to taking a look into the future. It
made Angie's father furious. It was a lot of superstitious nonsense, he said. Educated people
shouldn't have anything to do with those old
ways. And he wanted his children to be educated.
But Aunt Carlota was a kind and gentle person,
and Angie liked her. If she was a *curandera* as well,
that was fine with Angie.

"Will you come?" Aunt Carlota asked.

"I can't. I've got a date," Nita said, digging into
her pizza. "Sorry."

Angie shook her head. "I can't make it tonight,
either," she said. She leaned forward with the
same conspiratorial smile. "Don't tell Dad, but I'm
seeing Brad tonight."

She glanced at the clock. It was almost seven.
Brad would be along pretty soon. He always ate
dinner at the Pizzeria, and he always got plenty of
extra pizza if he wanted it, no charge, as long as
Gwen, her boss, wasn't looking.

18

Angie and Brad Rayburn hadn't been dating long, and she'd been happy since the beginning. Brad was so low-key and easygoing. He treated her well and always told her how beautiful she was and how much he cared for her.

"Your secret's safe with me," Aunt Carlota said with a smile. She knew about Angie and Brad, and if she disapproved, she didn't say so—unlike Angie's father, who had a fit when he found out his daughter was getting involved with an unemployed musician.

Juanita smiled at her. "So what do you want me to tell Dad tonight?"

Angie sighed. "I guess you can tell him I'm at Susan's, helping with her new apartment." She didn't like lying to her father, but if that was the only way she could see Brad, well, she had to do it. Angie wasn't a rebel, but she figured that people ought to be able to do what they wanted to do. And that went for Brad and his music, too. She wasn't that into Brad's sound, but if he was, and he didn't make her hang out with his strange musician friends, that was fine with her.

"Well, I hope you have a nice time. Stop by and see me when you can," Aunt Carlota said.

"I'll come by in the morning," Angie said. She glanced over her shoulder toward the kitchen. Gwen always managed to show up at the worst times and give her waitresses that I-know-you've-

19

been-goofing-off-and-I-don't-like-it look. "I guess I'd better get back to work before I get in trouble." She said good-bye and went back into the kitchen, where a rack of pizzas was coming out of the oven. As she began slicing one, Susan came up behind her.

"Angie, did you watch the Channel Five late news last night?"

Angie turned around. "No," she said. "The TV was on, but Dad was watching the Astros game. Why?"

"I still don't get that report I saw about that grave on the beach."

"Sorry, Susan." Angela shook her head. "I don't know any more about it than Freddie did. I know I didn't see anything in the paper about it this morning."

"Oh," Susan said absently. She looked around. "Where is Freddie, anyway?"

Angela started slicing another pizza. "I saw her go into the dining room a minute ago." She smiled a little. "That guy's back."

Susan brushed back an escaped strand of brown hair and tried to tuck it into her braid. "What guy?" she asked, slightly distracted.

"Don't you remember? It's all she talked about last week. The guy with the dark glasses who's been flirting with her." Once Angie and Brad had gotten serious, she'd stopped noticing the cute customers. But this one had caught her attention, mainly because he'd never taken his sunglasses off. Which was a little strange, she thought. The dining room was pretty dark, even in the afternoon. She guessed he thought sunglasses made him look cool.

"Oh, yeah, *that* one." Susan raised an eyebrow. "Are you sure that it wasn't Freddie who was flirting with him, instead of the other way around?"

"She probably was," Angie said with a grin. "So what else is new, huh?"

At that moment Freddie came into the kitchen. She was smiling a strange half smile, and her eyes were glazed over, as if she were sleepwalking. She bumped into a table, and a pitcher of water rocked and nearly tumbled over.

"Hey, watch where you're going, Freddie," Susan said, grabbing the pitcher.

"Huh?" Freddie asked. Her eyes focused, and she looked around as if she'd just woken up. "Oh, wow, you guys," she breathed. "I'm in love! He's wonderful! We're going on a date. Tomorrow night. After the audition. I have an audition. And a date."

Angie stared at her. "Love? How can you be in love? You haven't even gone out with him yet."

"Are you sure it isn't heartburn instead of love?" Susan asked skeptically. "After all, you have been chowing on those jalapeños all day.

And what's this about an audition?"

Freddie wrinkled her nose. "Just because you're both too self-controlled ever to fall in love at first sight doesn't mean that *I* can't." She leaned forward eagerly. "Not only is this guy super-sexy and *extremely* cool, but he's got his own band! And guess what! His group's opening a club right here in Galveston!"

"His group?" Susan inquired. She scratched her head, pretending to be puzzled. "What kind of group? Social group? Study group?" She grinned. "A group of groupies? A group of guppies? A group—"

"Ha ha," Freddie cut in sarcastically. "You are *so* funny." She turned to Angie. "They call themselves Blood Brothers." She clapped her hands excitedly. "*And* they're looking for a lead vocalist! I'm going to audition tomorrow night. Before the beach party he's giving." She trilled a little tune. "He thinks I've got a great voice."

"How does he know?" Susan asked. "Did you hum a few bars of the menu?"

"Oh, Freddie," Angie exclaimed, feeling Freddie's excitement. "It's your big chance! See? I *told* you it was a good thing you didn't hit it off with Lenny."

"And not only a vocalist," Freddie rushed on, her eyes sparkling. "The Brothers are looking for a guitarist, too. I told him about Brad."

22

"You did?" Angie asked. She clapped her hands. "That's terrific!"

"Yeah. And he says he's eager to meet him," Freddie says. "He'd like him to audition right away. Like tomorrow night." She grabbed Angie's hand. "Hey, maybe we can combine the auditions and the date. Want to double?"

"I wish I could," Angie said. "But tomorrow night is my sister's sixteenth birthday party. Maybe after we—"

"Hang on a minute," Susan broke in. "Isn't it a little weird that a rock group is opening a club?"

"Maybe they've made a lot of money," Angie suggested, thinking how great it would be for Brad to get steady work. "Maybe they're tired of being on the road and they're ready to settle down." A job in an established club, right here in Galveston, would be a hundred times better than pickup work. Maybe her father wouldn't object so much if Brad had a job like that.

"But if they made a lot of money," Susan said, "we'd know about it. I mean, we'd have heard of them." She frowned. "Blood Brothers? Doesn't ring a bell."

"So since when have you been an expert on rock groups?" Freddie demanded. She leaned against the wall and fanned herself with her hand, closing her eyes dramatically. "Wow. I tell you guys, he is totally amazing!"

Susan stepped to the door and peered into the dining room. "So that's Santa Claus, huh? The guy with the black hair?"

Freddie came up behind her. "Yeah, that's him. Isn't he cute?"

"I don't know about this guy, Freddie," she said doubtfully. "Are you sure you want to get involved with somebody you're working for?"

Freddie bristled. "So what's wrong with that?"

"Do you really think getting involved with a Blood Brother is a good idea?"

"Just because you don't go for the name of his group—"

"It's not that," Susan said, looking troubled. "It doesn't feel . . . it doesn't feel right, somehow. He's spooky-looking."

Freddie grinned. "Yeah, he's spooky, all right," she said. "Gives me goose bumps. Even makes me feel dizzy when I get close to him, like in the movies." She closed her eyes with a dreamy sigh. "This guy is so sexy. I can't believe he's for real."

Angie stepped to the door to see for herself. The guy was sitting at table twenty-two, in the farthest, darkest corner. The dining room was gloomy, as usual, and she could barely make out his face. She leaned forward. He looked younger than she would have thought, for somebody who had made enough money to buy a club. Late teens, probably. His face was lean and high-cheekboned, and his jaw was cut in a firm, sharp line. His black hair was swept back, and his eyebrows were a straight, dark slash across his face. He was wearing dark glasses and a black T-shirt. As she watched, his head swiveled in her direction, as if he was aware that she was studying him.

Angie swallowed. No wonder Freddie had gone overboard. Once you started looking at this guy, it was hard to look away. At the same time, there was something else. Something that made you *want* to look away. She shivered. Of course, she hadn't had a lot of experience with guys. Her father had seen to that. Maybe that was it. Maybe this guy was totally ordinary, and she was overreacting. She turned away from the door.

"So, Freddie," Angie said, "what's this guy's name?"

"His name?" Freddie asked dreamily.

"His *name*," Susan said. She snapped her fingers in front of Freddie's face. "You know, what people call him when they want to get his attention. Or when they say yes after he's asked them for a date."

"Oh, yeah." Freddie sighed. She straightened up. "It's Flint."

"Flint?" Angie asked.

"I think it fits," Susan said with a shrug.

"Well," Freddie said, "at least I've got an audition and a date. What have you got?"

Susan looked at her watch. "I've got seven o'clock," she said. "Time for us to get on the register, Angie." She grinned at Freddie, who was still too distracted to notice. "Hang in there, Juliet."

Four

Brad Rayburn leaned across the counter at the cash register as Angie took his order. In a couple of minutes she'd bring him a large pizza, double cheese and everything but anchovies, just the way he liked it. Not bad for two bucks.

Brad grinned. He knew that in the beginning Angie had felt uneasy about their little arrangement. She didn't like stealing, even if it was from a witch like Gwen. But when he'd pointed out that she got an all-you-want-to-eat lunch for free and that she never ate anything more than a little salad, she'd agreed that it was okay. He was taking her lunch, that was all. Angie was so crazy about him that if he could justify things, he could usually get Angie to go along with anything.

Well, almost anything.

Angie was saying something to him, half whispering as she handed him the change from his five. Brad wasn't listening. His grin had changed into a small frown. He took the coins, letting his eyes linger on Angie's pretty throat, where the gold chain of her crucifix disappeared under her blouse. You'd think, when a girl had a body like Angie's, she'd show it a little more. Not that he was after only one thing with Angie. She had a lot going for her, like those terrific big brown eyes, and her graceful, hip-swaying walk, and the soft, sweet way she had of letting him know that he was somebody special. And she was fun to hang around with.

Angie was still talking when Brad tuned her back in. "Sorry," he said, smiling. "Guess I wasn't paying attention. At least not to what you were saying."

Angie got his point and blushed. "I said," she whispered breathlessly, "that the guy over in the corner is opening a club here in Galveston. He's got a band called Blood Brothers. He told Freddie they're looking for a guitarist. He wants to talk to you about an audition."

That got his attention. He stared at her. "An audition?" he asked incredulously. "No kidding! How'd he find out about me?"

"Freddie told him," Angie said. Gwen was

coming out of the kitchen, and she stepped back hurriedly, raising her voice. "Your pizza will be out in a minute, sir. Please have a seat and I'll bring you your drink."

Brad turned around, squinting in the dim light. The guy at the back table smiled at him and raised his hand in a lazy, beckoning gesture. He wore dark glasses, which wasn't too odd, considering he was a rocker. Not only did musicians tend to be a bit eccentric, but they could be hard to get along with, too. That was why he'd been out of a job for the past couple of months—because the leader of the last band he'd worked with had been such a jerk that nobody could get along with him. Brad had given Angie some story about his style not matching the band's. Musical integrity, he'd called it. But the truth, plain and simple, was that they had fired him for missing too many rehearsals.

"Hello, Bradley," the guy with the dark glasses said as Brad reached his table. His voice was mellow—smooth and deep. A baritone. Probably lead vocalist as well as head honcho. "I believe you're the man I've been waiting for."

"Oh, yeah?" Brad asked carelessly. He sat down, careful not to betray any eagerness. In this business you played it close to the heart. You didn't give away any advantage. "Brad," he said. He hated being called Bradley. "My name's Brad."

29

The guy smiled slightly, as if he were amused at something. "Flint," he said.

Brad stirred uneasily as Angie set a glass down in front of him, smiled, and disappeared again. "Okay," he said. "Flint." It was those glasses. Brad couldn't see the guy's eyes. He liked to be able to see the person he was talking to, see whether his eyes and his mouth were telling the same story. He shifted again. "So what makes you think we can do business?" he asked. "What kind of music are you into?"

Flint didn't answer his question. "I understand," he said softly, "that you play guitar." His voice was oddly accented. Maybe he was some kind of foreigner. European, maybe. They had some hot groups in Germany. England, too. "I understand that you are a very good guitar player."

Brad turned the cold glass in his fingers. "Yeah," he said. "*Lead* guitar." No point in letting this guy Flint get the idea that he'd do backup work—although he probably would, if it meant steady work. But that wasn't the way you started negotiating. You started at the top. That way you were in control.

"That's good," Flint said approvingly. "I would be interested in hearing you play, Bradley. My group is called Blood Brothers."

Brad shrugged. "Original name," he said. The last group had called themselves Bad News. And that's exactly what they turned out to be. He leaned forward. "What kind of music do you do?" If they weren't in the same groove, this was a waste of time.

"Our name is unique," Flint replied, "as is our music." He smiled then. Or rather, he stretched his lips across his teeth. Brad wasn't sure if it was a smile or not, since he couldn't see the eyes. "I can guarantee," he added, "that you will find working with us far more rewarding than your last employment. Infinitely more rewarding." The smile again, if that's what it was. "I can almost guarantee, Bradley, that you will not be forced to leave us."

Brad scowled, forgetting his question about the music. "Did Freddie tell you that?" he asked. His scowl deepened. He didn't think Freddie even knew about his getting fired, but the music scene in Galveston was pretty small, and word could have gotten around.

"No. Frederica didn't tell me. Nobody had to tell me," Flint said. He leaned back in his chair and gracefully stroked his black hair. His fingers were long and thin, the nails carefully manicured and sharply pointed.

Brad wiped the palms of his hands on his jeans. This entire exchange was making him more than a little nervous.

Not raising his voice, Flint went on. "Furthermore, Bradley, I am quite certain that should you decide to join our group, you will find yourself anxious to practice with us. I do not foresee the regularity and quality of your participation being an issue for concern."

Brad blinked. Definitely a foreigner. People around Galveston didn't talk like that. Who was this guy? And how did he know so much about Brad? He was beginning to feel very uncomfortable. Maybe he'd better—

"Don't bother yourself about it, Bradley," Flint said. He leaned forward and touched Brad's hand with one long finger. "It is of no consequence."

Suddenly Brad found himself agreeing. Whatever had been on his mind—bad news, good news—it wasn't important. What was important now was that this guy Flint was offering him the possibility of work. Real work. That would make Angie happy. Maybe, if the job turned out to be steady, she'd agree to get an apartment with him. Of course, she'd probably want to be engaged first, but he could handle that. If he had a regular gig, he could handle just about anything, no sweat.

"Sure, Flint," he said easily. "Yeah, you're right. A hundred percent right. Say, what about that audition, huh? And what's this about a club you're buying? Here in Galveston?" It was the right place, that was for sure. Lots of teens with nothing to do came down from Houston every weekend, looking for action. Big-money teens. You could tell by the sports cars, dune buggies, and big-wheel pickups that jammed the beach. Brad smiled. If he had a regular gig, maybe he'd get a sports car too.

Flint nodded. "Yes, Bradley. That is correct. In Galveston. Our new club will be called Dark of the Moon." He smiled. "We are, shall we say, targeting the teenage audience. Particularly the tourists. You will be available for an audition tomorrow night?"

It was more of a statement than a question. Brad seemed to remember that Angie had been planning something, but he couldn't quite think what it was. "That's cool," he said. He figured he could reschedule whatever it was that Angie had been planning.

"Perhaps," Flint said, spreading his hands on the table in front of him, "we could arrange a small party before the audition. A beach party, say, for some of your friends and some of mine."

"Hey, yeah," Brad said. "A beach party."

"Fine," Flint said. "Around eight? There is a nice spot on East Beach Drive. I will arrange for the food and drink. After the party we will hold your audition at the house my group has rented."

Brad frowned, still trying to remember what it was that he and Angie had been planning. Whatever it was, it probably wasn't too important, or he wouldn't have forgotten it. Anyway, he couldn't very well say no to a party before his big

33

chance, could he? Of course not. That would be just plain stupid.

"Frederica has already agreed to come," Flint said. "Would you please see to it that Susan is there as well? I have a friend who would very much like to meet her. And, of course, you will bring Angela. Even though she doesn't swim, I'm sure she will enjoy the evening."

The skin prickled on the back of Brad's neck. Angie hated that she couldn't swim. It wasn't something she bragged about. "Hey, how do you know so much about us?" he demanded. "I mean, if you're new in town, how'd you find out about—"

Flint touched Brad's hand again. "These questions are not important," he admonished in a soft, reassuring voice. "Just be sure Angela comes with you."

Brad found that he had no more questions.

"But, Brad," Angie objected, feeling frustrated, "we *can't* go to the beach tomorrow night!" She leaned back against the car seat and looked out at the silvery glaze of moonlight on the water of the bay. She and Brad were parked at their favorite spot, where they could see a long stretch of quiet beach, deserted now in the moonlight. "It's Juanita's sixteenth birthday party. I don't see how you could have forgotten. I'm even getting off work early so I can help out."

A look of surprise crossed Brad's face, and Angie knew that he really had forgotten about the party. But he didn't like to admit that he'd made a mistake.

"Yeah, but this guy's offering me an audition. This is the break I've been waiting for."

"That's another thing we need to talk about," Angie said. She bit her lip. She really wanted Brad to find a job that he liked. But there was something about Flint that made her feel terribly uncomfortable. The more she thought about it, the more she felt . . . well, afraid. She knew that was pretty silly, and it certainly wasn't something she could say to Brad. "Are you sure about playing with him? I mean, do you even know what he and his band are really about?" she asked. She wished she could think of a good reason to ask him to look for a different gig.

"Am I sure?" Brad laughed. "You've got to be kidding, Angie. The Brothers and me—we're going to make sweet music together." He leaned toward her and ran his finger tenderly down her neck. "Like you and me, huh? We make sweet music together."

Angie closed her eyes, pushing Flint out of her mind. She loved it when Brad touched her softly like that. Now, as he pulled her gently toward him, she went willingly into his arms, lifting her lips to his.

After a moment Brad nuzzled her neck. "About tomorrow night," he said softly.

Angie sighed. "I can't," she said. "My folks expect me to help. It would mean a lot to Juanita for me to be there. And it would mean a lot to me for you to be there."

"We don't have to stay all evening, do we?" Brad asked, punctuating each word with a gentle kiss on Angie's face. "Listen, couldn't we slip out around eight? By that time everyone else will be there, and we can leave without hurting your sister's feelings."

Angie frowned doubtfully. "I don't know if that's a good idea, Brad. I promised. And I have to help clean up after—"

"You'll never be missed, I guarantee," Brad interrupted. "There'll be so many guys there, Nita won't even know you're gone. And I'll have you back by nine thirty. How's that, huh? You'll be back for cleanup time." He bent down to kiss her again.

"Well," Angie said slowly after their lips parted, "I guess, if it's only for a little while—"

Brad gave her a sly grin. "You can wear your new red bikini."

Angie felt alarmed. "I told you I could never wear that bikini for anybody else but you," she protested. Just thinking about the way she looked in the skimpy swimsuit made her blush.

36

"For anybody but me and a few friends," Brad said soothingly. He pulled her close again. "Listen, I just want to show you off a little. I want them to see what a wonderful girlfriend I've got. You don't mind if I feel that way about you, do you? That I'm so happy you're mine?"

Angie minded. What she and Brad had together was very precious to her. But it was also very private, and she wanted to keep it that way. She didn't like the idea of wearing her bikini in front of Flint—or the rest of the Blood Brothers, for that matter. She didn't want these people to get the wrong idea about her. "Anyway," Brad added confidently, "it'll be a good time. Freddie's going to be there, and Susan, too."

"Susan?" Angie asked, surprised. She'd known about Freddie, who'd had a date with Flint, plus the audition. But Susan hadn't mentioned anything about coming to the party.

"Yeah," Brad replied. "Flint said he had a friend who wanted to meet her, so I stopped off in the kitchen tonight while I was waiting for you and asked her. She wasn't exactly thrilled, but she said she'd come when I told her you'd be there too."

"I wonder," Angie said thoughtfully, "how Flint's friend even knew about Susan. I mean, when did he see her?"

Brad shrugged. "Who knows? Maybe he stopped in at the Pizzeria, took a look, and liked what he saw." He grinned. "Or maybe he staked out her house." He trailed his finger down Angie's cheek to her neck, then bent toward her and kissed the hollow of her throat, where her blouse opened. "Who cares?" he whispered.

Angie took a deep breath and tensed herself to pull away. She knew where this was leading. But before she could move, Brad reached up and pulled the comb out of her hair. It tumbled down over her shoulders.

"All I care about is you, Angie," he said in a husky voice. "You drive me crazy, you know that? Your body, your skin, your hair—" He kissed her again, his fingers reaching for the buttons of her blouse.

Angie shivered, loving his lips, the touch of his fingers. But at the same time she knew that the feeling was dangerous. She shouldn't be doing this. It might be old-fashioned, but that's the way she'd been raised.

"No, Brad," she whispered urgently. She pushed his hands away and pulled back from him. "Please don't."

"But, Angie," Brad said, reaching for her again. "It would be so wonderful, you and me together."

Angie shook her head. They'd been through this over and over again. Why couldn't he understand?

She glanced at her watch. "I've got to get home, Brad. It's nearly ten, and Mom worries if

I'm not back at the end of my shift."

Brad leaned back in the seat, heaving an audible, frustrated sigh.

Angie twisted her hair up and thrust the comb through the knot at the back of her neck. "Maybe," she said, changing the subject, "the job with the Brothers will work out."

Brad nodded. "Yeah," he said. "With a few paychecks under my belt, things are gonna be different. Hey, maybe then we can get a place together. Makes sense, doesn't it? Going halves on the rent? That way we'd be able to afford something close to the beach."

Angela's mouth tightened. She really cared about Brad, but how could she reject everything her parents had taught her and move in with him, without any real commitment—a guarantee that he wouldn't move out on her a few months later? For her it was too big a risk, too important a decision. Before she dared to do such a thing, she had to be sure that Brad was as serious about their relationship as she was. She wasn't sure about that at all—at least not yet.

"You know how I feel, Brad," she said quietly. "Love isn't something to be taken lightly. For two people to do that, they have to know for certain—"

Brad turned the key in the ignition. "Yeah, I know," he broke in. He grinned at her. "We'll see how things turn out, okay?"

Angie sighed as they drove off. If she was waiting for a commitment, she'd have to wait a while longer.

Five

───────────

"Well, here it is," Susan said. "Home sweet home." She turned the key in the lock and stepped into her darkened apartment with Freddie a pace behind her.

"Hey, nice," Freddie said, looking around. "I'm impressed."

Susan laughed. "And you haven't even seen it with the lights on yet."

For a moment she stood by the door in the half dark, admiring the way the moonlight fell through the open window and across the floor. Now that she had the furniture arranged the way she wanted it, the room looked good, especially with the moonlight turning the gauzy curtains to silver and etching a silver puddle on the floor.

Freddie went to the window. "Hey, look, a view," she said, laughing. "A formal garden and a beach." The window looked out on Betty's small vegetable plot and the kids' sandbox.

Susan flicked on the light switch, and the room sprang to life. "What I like best about it," she said, "is that it's mine. My own private place. It isn't very big, but I love coming in and closing the door behind me, knowing I can be all alone." She grinned at Freddie. "Or invite a friend over," she added. Freddie had followed her home to borrow a cover-up for tomorrow night's beach party.

Freddie lowered herself into the chair with the saggy cushion. "Yeah. I wish I could have my own place too. Maybe I will next year, if I can make enough money. And if I can talk Mom into it."

Freddie's mother ran the Holiday Plaza, a motel over on Holiday Drive. She and Freddie had a large suite of rooms on the second floor. Susan sometimes felt sorry for Freddie. Her mother was always so busy with the motel that she didn't have much time for her daughter.

"Of course," Freddie added, "if this singing job with Flint and the Brothers comes through, maybe I'll make *lots* of money." She held up both hands. Her fingers were crossed. "I could even get my own suite at my mom's place," Freddie joked.

"Maybe," Susan said, trying to sound enthusiastic. For some reason Flint made her feel uneasy, which was kind of odd, because she hadn't even met him. Flint was certainly good-looking, in a dark, brooding sort of way. She could see that when he sat in the back of the Pizzeria. But there was something else, something she couldn't quite put her finger on. Maybe he looked too smooth. Maybe Freddie was already too infatuated with him. Whatever it was, she felt uncomfortable.

Freddie gave a dreamy sigh and swung her legs over the arm of the chair. "How lucky can a girl get?" she asked. "An audition—*and* a date."

"Yeah, how lucky," Susan said dryly. She wasn't looking forward to tomorrow night's party. At least Freddie and Angie would be there, and Brad was all right. And it *was* time she got out and had a little fun. With the job and moving she'd been so busy lately that she hadn't had time even to think about partying.

She looked down at her watch, seeing with some surprise that it was already ten o'clock.

"Mind if I turn on the television?" she asked. "I want to catch the follow-up on last night's story about that grave on the beach." Was that it, or did she really just want to see Drew Morris again? She'd thought about him several times that day, in a strange, anticipatory way. If she didn't know better, she'd almost think she was falling in love with him. But that was ridiculous. You didn't fall in love with somebody you saw on television—at least, not if you were practical, down-to-earth Susan Scott.

"Oh, you mean that story that nobody else knows anything about? Be my guest," Freddie replied. She ruffled her coppery hair and settled back into the couch. "Wake me up when they show the invisible blood," she added, closing her eyes.

"I'm having a sandwich. Want one?" Susan asked. "I have lemonade too."

Freddie's eyes didn't open. "Sure," she said. "Sounds great. In the meantime I think I'll catch a few z's."

Susan flicked on the TV. The Channel Five anchorwoman was already on, doing a story about the annual Muscle Beach Extravaganza. Susan went into the kitchen, where the sound of the newscast was a background to her thoughts. She wasn't really listening, though. She was thinking about Drew Morris. When she realized what she was doing, she forced herself to stop. She had to admit that if it wasn't love, at least it was a pretty heavy crush.

The weatherman was finishing his report as Susan returned to the living room. She got out her new place mats and napkins, thinking about Drew Morris's story from the evening before. She frowned a little as she went back into the kitchen for the sandwiches and lemonade. She wondered if the story would be on again tonight, or if she really had imagined it all. If the TV news crew had been out there on the beach, you'd think Freddie would have run into them. It wasn't easy to miss a sound truck and a camera crew and all those lights.

In fact, the whole thing had been on Susan's mind all day—so much so that at three in the afternoon, when she got her lunch break, she'd hopped in the car and driven over to the beach. She parked on East Beach Drive, in front of the SeaWall Condos, and walked along the beach for a hundred yards or so. She hadn't seen anything. And when she got back to the Pizzeria, the evening paper was on the newsstand, without a word about the police digging up the grave. It was really weird; it was as if it had never happened. But Susan knew it had. She could never have dreamed up Drew Morris's compelling eyes or his urgent voice. No, what she had seen on the television the night before had been real. The strange thing was that it didn't seem to connect with anything else.

"Here's your sandwich," Susan said, and Freddie's eyes popped open.

"Great," she said enthusiastically as she swung her legs down. "Thanks." She looked at the TV, where the sportscaster was wrapping up his baseball report. "Did I miss anything important?"

"Not unless you were betting on the Astros," Susan replied with a laugh. "They lost to the Braves in the bottom of the ninth." She sat down on the sofa as the anchorwoman came back on the screen. "Now for our final report of the evening—" she began.

The lights suddenly dimmed. "Hey! What's going on?" Freddie asked.

"That happened last night, too," Susan said, frowning.

"Maybe you ought to ask Mack about it," Freddie said.

"I plan to, once he gets back from El Paso. I also want to get some candles, in case Mack doesn't get back soon enough," Susan added.

"Yeah, candles." Freddie munched her sandwich. "It's hurricane season, you know. Mom bought a bunch last week. And canned food, too. You ought to stock plenty of canned stuff." She grinned. "Hey, now that you've got your own place, we could have a hurricane party here. What do you think about that?"

But Susan wasn't listening. She was leaning forward, watching the television, her sandwich forgotten in her hand. Drew Morris was standing in front of a motel, speaking into a microphone. His handsome face was pale and more drawn than it had been the night before, and it seemed lined with sadness. His pale gray-green eyes were fastened on

46

Susan's with an intensity that made her tremble.

"Our live report tonight," he said slowly, "is from a motel, in southeast Galveston, on Holiday Drive."

"Hey!" Freddie exclaimed. She thumped her glass down on the table. "That's our motel!"

"A body has been found," Drew Morris went on soberly. "That makes the second body in two days in this seaside town. Not in a sandy grave this time, but in a bed on the second floor of the motel behind me. The victim here is a young woman in her early twenties. The coroner has not yet determined a cause of death, and police are withholding her identity. Last night, if you recall, the body of a young man was found in a shallow grave on the beach not far from here." His voice deepened, and Susan thought it was filled with an inexpressible sadness. "The question we now have to ask is *why*. Why did these two young people lose their lives? Is there a connection between these two seemingly unrelated tragedies? Will other deaths follow? And who will be next?"

Susan dropped her sandwich onto her plate and twisted her fingers together, her mouth suddenly bone-dry. Those gray-green eyes held hers, connecting the two of them in some sort of inexplicable bond. A powerful force, coming from him, seemed to surge through her. She once again was sure that the reporter was speaking directly to her, as if he wanted to—*had* to—have an answer. An answer from Susan, as if Susan somehow held the key to the mystery he was reporting. The urgency of his questions pulsed through her.

"These are the questions that must be answered," Drew Morris repeated, his voice emphatic, low, taut. His eyes looked tormented, as if he were searching some bleak horizon for the truth, but finding only clouds and darkness. "Why? And who? Who will be next?"

"Whoa," Freddie muttered, shaking her head. "This is *weird*. I mean, this is *really* weird." She rose from her chair. "Where's your phone? I'm going to call my mom and see if she's okay."

"In the kitchen," Susan said, her eyes still on the screen. But Drew Morris's face had faded away, and she got up and turned off the television set. Then she went to the window and looked out. But with the light behind her, all she could see was her own pale face reflected in the dark glass.

She closed her eyes. Even though she knew it wasn't rational, she still couldn't shake the feeling that the reporter had been speaking to her, and to her alone, as if his story were a report that *she*, of all the tens of thousands of viewers, had to hear. She bit her lip. Maybe she should call the station and ask for Drew Morris. Maybe she should talk to him and find out why—

Then she caught herself, and her eyes flew

open. This was ridiculous. It was crazy! Drew Morris was only a good-looking reporter—with eyes she happened to find attractive—doing a job. It happened that he'd drawn two tough assignments, one after the other, and maybe he'd gotten too deeply involved with the stories. That happened sometimes. It would account for the tormented intensity of his gaze. Sure, that was it. Any reporter would be likely to feel an interest in two cases like these. And the connection she felt with him? Well, that was her imagination working overtime, that's all it was. Fantasy. A fiction.

In the window, as in a mirror, she saw Freddie come out of the kitchen wearing a puzzled expression.

"Crazy," she muttered. "Weird. Wacko."

"What?" Susan asked, turning around.

"Didn't that reporter say he was doing a live spot?" Freddie demanded.

Susan nodded. "Yeah. So?"

"So Mom swears there's no TV crew," Freddie said. "Not earlier, not now. I made her go out and look." She scowled. "I *know* it was our motel. They didn't show the sign, but I saw that stupid tilted palm tree out front that leans like the Tower of Pisa. I keep telling Mom to get it cut before it falls on some tourist."

Susan felt the skin prickling on the back of her neck. "There wasn't any sign of the TV cameras

49

on the beach last night, either," she said quietly. It was as if Drew Morris were a figure from an unknown dimension, suddenly visible on her television set.

Freddie shook her head. "Listen, would you mind if I borrowed that beach cover-up and drove on home?" she asked. "I mean, I hate to eat and run, but this thing has me curious. I'd like to know what's going on."

Susan headed for the closet. "So would I." If Mack were here, instead of on vacation in El Paso, she could ask him. He was a cop—he'd know. But he and the family wouldn't be back until tomorrow.

"I'll call you if I find anything out," Freddie promised, taking the cover-up from Susan. "Anyway, I'll see you at work in the morning." She grinned. "And don't forget our triple date tomorrow night."

Susan wrinkled her nose. "I don't know about this, Freddie. I think I might change my mind. I'm not exactly crazy about the whole idea."

"Don't you dare," Freddie said. "I need you for moral support. Tomorrow night's a big night for me."

Susan grinned. "Oh, yeah? And are you worried about your morals?"

"Some friend you are," Freddie said affectionately. "You'll be there? Please?"

"I guess," Susan said. She smiled. "For you."

"Hey, aren't you even curious about this guy who wants to meet you?"

"Maybe," Susan admitted. "Yeah, a little. But not enough to make me want to spend an evening with"—she was going to say "with Flint" but thought better of it—"with a bunch of people I don't know," she amended.

"It'll do you good," Freddie said breezily. "You don't go out often enough."

Susan sighed. This was an argument they had at least once a week. "Thanks for the advice," she said. "I'll keep it in mind the next time two or three guys ask me out." It was what she always said.

"The reason they don't," Freddie said, "is that you're too serious. You've got to lighten up."

"Yeah," Susan said. "I'll work on it."

Freddie gave her a hug. "See you tomorrow," she said, and banged the door shut behind her.

Feeling restless, Susan turned on the TV for a few minutes and watched a sitcom. Then she turned the set off and went into the kitchen to put away the dishes and check the lock on the back door. In the living room again, she turned off the light and sat on the sofa, watching the moonlight stream through the window. Thinking of Drew Morris, and of his eyes still fastened relentlessly on hers, Susan could feel him gaze at her from the silvery shadows. Again she felt the sense of urgency that had pulsed through her when he spoke. She heard his voice, his questions, echoing in her head.

Why?

Who?

And who would be next?

Six

―――――――――
⟨ornament⟩

Freddie trudged through the warm sand, shaking the water out of her hair. She glanced up and down the beach. In one direction, toward Galveston, she could see the expensive condominiums rising like tall glass towers. In the other was the concession stand at Apffel Park. Ahead lay the dunes, shadowy in the deepening twilight, and the fire the guys had built. Behind her was the ocean, flat and calm, growing dark. Down at Stewart Park, on the other side of the condos, there was plenty of noise and bright light, and the beach was crowded, even at night. But here the beach was secluded and quiet, nothing but sand and sky and water.

Susan sat up and tossed her a towel. "How was the water?"

"Great!" Freddie said. She toweled herself off and flopped down on the blanket beside Susan. She sighed again. "The whole evening has been terrific. The audition was wonderful, the Brothers are out of this world, Flint is . . ." She looked out into the water, where Flint was swimming around like a dolphin, flashing in and out of the surf.

"You seem to have run out of adjectives," Susan said quietly.

"Well, you might too," Freddie replied, "if you could bring yourself to spend some time with him. You know, talk to him, get to know him." She knew that Susan wasn't wild about Flint, but she didn't have to ignore him completely, did she?

"You may be right," Susan said. "I really haven't given him—or any of the other guys either, for that matter—a fair chance. I'm sorry if I'm ruining your good time."

"That's okay," Freddie said. "You're not."

Susan didn't reply. Freddie saw that her eyes were on Bishop, the guy who had asked to meet her. He was out in the deep water with Brad, beyond the surf. Freddie grinned a little. Bishop was blond and good-looking. If she hadn't seen Flint first, she might have fallen for Bishop. Or even Russel or Sid, the other two Brothers, neither of whom had come to the beach party. They were both super-cute too. The Brothers probably found themselves surrounded by love-struck groupies all

54

the time. That was okay, she thought, chuckling to herself, as long as *she* held the inside track.

On the other side of Susan, Angie sat up, adjusting the top of her skimpy red swimsuit. Freddie had to smile at that, too. Angie was obviously nervous about that bikini. Bishop's low, admiring whistle hadn't helped the situation.

"So they hired you?" Angie asked.

"Yeah," Freddie said happily. "Of course, it's only week to week for a while, until they see how I do. But it's a chance."

"How did you like it?" Susan asked. "The music, I mean."

Freddie frowned a little. "Well, it's going to take some getting used to," she said. "I'll have to adjust my style a little. But I guess that happens with any new group."

She hadn't known what to expect when she went into the audition earlier that evening. For one thing, she'd thought Brad was going to be there, but as it turned out, they were auditioning separately. His would come later that evening. But the big news was the Brothers' music. Technically, it was very unusual, based on the synthesizers Flint and Bishop played. There was a heavy, deep rhythm of bass and drums. They worked in minor keys, too, which gave the music an eerie quality. And then there were the lyrics.

"Adjust how?" Susan wanted to know.

"That's hard to say." Freddie really couldn't explain. Singing with the Brothers, she had done things with her voice that she hadn't known she could do. She'd felt the music's energy in a new way. But it was a scary energy, dark, so powerful . . . She frowned. She didn't want to try to explain. They'd think she'd gone totally flaky. But Susan and Angie were waiting for an explanation. "I guess it's the kind of music you feel in your gut," she said finally. "It's kind of, well, mesmerizing. The lyrics especially. They're sort of . . ." She paused, searching for the right word. "I don't know, seductive."

Susan began folding the beach towels. "Seductive, huh?" She laughed a little. "Sounds dangerous."

Seductive, yes, Freddie thought, poking her toes into the sand. When she sang with the Brothers, it was as if all her own energy, her own soul, somehow drained from her, so that she was charged entirely by the music. In fact, she'd been surprised—and a little scared—at the way it had pushed her to go beyond her limits. Beyond her range, which ordinarily wasn't anything spectacular. The power even took her beyond her technical ability.

"Sing something for us," Angie said.

"I can't," Freddie said.

"How come?" Susan asked. "Did you have to sign a pledge? No singing outside the club?"

"No. I can't remember any of the songs," Freddie said simply. That was weird, too. She had a good memory. She always remembered lyrics, especially when they were powerful, as the Brothers' were.

"Too bad," Angie said.

"Yeah," Freddie said, making her tone lighter. "Well, I guess you'll just have to come to the club and listen." She squared her shoulders. When she really got going with the Brothers, when she knew the lyrics better, she'd like it a lot more. Right now it was probably just a matter of not being familiar with the mood, the rhythm. And not being quite sure what the Brothers wanted from her.

Susan nodded. "We'll be there," she said. "In the front row." She changed the subject. "What did you find out last night when you got home? About the girl they found dead in the motel, I mean."

"A dead girl in the motel?" Angie asked, startled. "What happened? Who was she?"

"There wasn't any dead girl," Freddie said.

Susan straightened up. "But we saw—"

"I know what we saw," Freddie said, "or at least what we thought we saw. But I'm telling you what I saw. There were no TV crews, no cops, no dead girl—" She shrugged. "I guess we made a mistake. The only explanation is that there's some other motel on Holiday Drive with a leaning palm tree out front. I guess I've never noticed it. Either that or there was something funny about that lemonade you gave me."

Susan was looking troubled, but she only said, "Yeah, I guess you're right. About another motel, that is. I'm still curious about the grave on the beach, though."

Freddie saw her looking down the beach, toward the condos. That's where she had said the grave was supposed to have been. Freddie couldn't quite put it all together. The grave on the beach and the dead girl in the motel—

"What time is it?" Angie asked Susan.

"Nine fifteen," Susan said, looking at her watch.

"Oops," Angie said. She scrambled to her feet and waved at Brad. "I've got to get back to Nita's party. It'll be time to clean up the mess."

"I'm ready to go," Susan said. "Want me to take you home? It'll give Brad a little time to get ready for his audition."

"Thanks," Angie said, and began to pull her jeans and shirt on over her dry suit. Freddie suspected that her parents, who were on the strict side, didn't know that she even owned a bikini.

Susan stood up. "Are you going over to Flint's for Brad's audition?" she asked Freddie.

"I wasn't invited," Freddie said. She looked up. The three guys were coming toward them from the water, bodies sleek and shiny. Flint and Bishop were wearing their dark glasses. That struck her as funny, and she giggled. Boy, how cool could you get? She turned to Susan. "I heard Bishop asked you out."

Susan nodded.

"Well, what did you say?"

"I said no thank you," Susan replied evenly. She glanced toward the guys. "Bishop isn't exactly my type" she added, in a lower voice.

"The trouble with you, Susan," Freddie said, "is that you're just too picky. What's wrong with Bishop?"

Susan shrugged. "I'll let you know when I've figured it out myself," she said. "In the meantime let's just say that I'm not likely to be the Brothers' greatest fan." She grinned at Freddie. "Although I can't wait to hear *you* sing, after they've opened the club."

For once he hadn't been upset that Angie had to leave early. The beach party had been fun, Brad thought, taking his electric guitar out of the case, but he'd been glad when it was time to break it up. Angie had seemed on edge all evening. She was probably upset about missing her sister's party and couldn't let go and enjoy herself. Susan had been kind of a wet blanket, too, and Brad had no idea what her problem was. But Flint and Bishop were great. He grinned. In fact, he hadn't come across such friendly, interesting guys in a long time. And that was good. It was important to like the guys you worked with.

He'd also managed to find out quite a bit about the Blood Brothers while they'd been partying. They'd been playing up in Dallas for a while, apparently. That's where they lost both their lead vocalist and their guitarist. Then Flint had come into some money—an inheritance of some kind—and they'd decided to relocate and start up their own club. They were calling it the Dark of the Moon. But before they could open, they had to find replacements for the band members who had left. That's where he came in.

Lucky for the Brothers he was available, Brad thought confidently. He carried his guitar into the house. He reminded himself that it probably wasn't cool to act too cocky. He didn't want them to think that he thought he had the job sewn up, even if it was true.

The house the Brothers had rented was a huge old Victorian, with high ceilings and big rooms, lots of them. It was a good house for a group like this, Brad decided. The guys lived upstairs, and downstairs there was plenty of room to store equipment and to practice. It was in the middle of town, but there weren't many houses on the block. The lots on both sides of the house were vacant, and there was a big cemetery across the street. No band could afford to have the neighbors calling the cops all the time because of loud music. In this business the dead made good neighbors. He grinned at his own joke.

The four Brothers, in black jeans, black tees, and dark glasses were already waiting for him in the practice room. Flint smiled and nodded at an empty stool, handing Brad a tall, cool glass. Brad took his place, beginning to feel a little nervous. But that was okay. A few nerves would pump up his adrenaline. He plugged in his instrument, gulped at the glass, and flexed his fingers. A lot was hanging on tonight. He had to be good.

He *was* good. After a few technical preliminaries about tempo, key, and so on, the group swung into the first number, pulling him with them. Brad had a good ear for melody and rhythm, and he picked the first song up easily. The group's sound was original. Actually, though, it wasn't really a sound. It was more like an effect, something he felt more than he heard. He felt it in his bones, in his blood, in some almost subliminal way.

All through that first number, Brad tried to stay on top of the music, to figure it out, the way he usually did when he sat in with a new group. He tried counting out the drum tempo, picking out the chord structure, and anticipating the melody—what there was of it. But that didn't work with these guys. The sound drifted and twisted, snakelike. It wasn't anything you could analyze. Anyway, his mind wasn't working too well. His brain kept disconnecting.

Sometime during the second number, though, he stopped worrying about contolling the sound. He found himself falling into the music, letting it flow through him and out of his fingers. That was when he got good. Very good. He got deep into the music. He stopped caring about being good or landing a job with the Brothers or even impressing Flint. He cared only about being part of the music, having it inside him, flowing in his veins like sweet, hot blood.

After the third or fourth number—who was counting?—Flint looked up from the synthesizer. He moved his head, and the rest of the Brothers stopped playing. They all looked at Brad.

"Yes," Flint said appreciatively. He reached out and touched Brad's arm with a smile. "Yes, indeed," he said. "I believe we have found our man." The other Brothers nodded in turn as Flint looked pointedly at each one.

Flint then took off his glasses, and Brad could see that his eyes were very dark, very deep, very expressive. His eyes had the music in them. He moved from behind the synthesizer and came closer.

After that the evening got really hazy. Brad

never could remember it, even when he tried.

"You've been staying out this late on a regular basis?"

Susan turned around, the key to her apartment in her hand. Mack was coming up the stairs behind her. He was still wearing his uniform, so he'd probably just gotten off duty. She smiled affectionately. Even if he was putting on his big-brother act in a major way, she was glad to see him—probably because he'd been away for two weeks.

"It's not even ten," Susan said defensively, opening the door. "How was El Paso?"

"Hot." Mack tossed his cap onto the coffee table and sat down heavily. "And dry. Like the desert." He glanced around. "Hey, not bad. You've got this place looking like home."

Susan was already in the kitchen. "Iced tea?" she called out.

"Please. Heavy on the ice."

In a moment Susan was back with the drinks. She switched on the TV. "I hope you don't mind," she said. "I've been following a news story." She sat down, intent on the television.

"Oh, yeah?" Mack asked lazily, sipping his tea. He kicked off his shoes. "Well, the newsroom's going to be busy tonight. They dug up some guy's body on the beach a few hours ago. And some girl turned up dead in a motel just as I was clocking out."

"What?" Susan asked. "But the girl in the motel—that was *last* night! And what did you say about a body on the beach?"

Her brother gestured at the set. "If you'll listen, you can hear all about it. Probably be the lead story."

The anchorwoman was looking at the camera, somber-faced. "Our top story tonight," she said, "is the discovery of a shallow grave on the beach, near the SeaWall Condominium. Police have uncovered the body of a young man. He has been identified as a Dallas television newsman named Drew Morris, who disappeared four days ago." On the screen flashed the face of a smiling young man, dark-haired, handsome. He had pale gray-green eyes.

Susan sucked in her breath, not believing. Her heart was thumping so loudly that she knew Mack must be able to hear it.

"Drew . . . Morris?" she whispered. She felt stunned, as if she had lost a friend. But behind that loss there was a deeper, darker fear. If Drew Morris was buried on the beach, who was the man on the TV screen the last two nights?

"Yeah, Morris, that's the guy," Mack said, leaning forward, his elbows on his knees. "Some guy from the condo was walking his dog on the beach about seven tonight. The dog dug up the grave."

The anchorwoman's sober face filled the screen

64

again. "Police have not yet identified the cause of Mr. Morris's death. Channel Seven in Dallas reports that he was in Galveston following a story involving the daughter of a prominent North Texas physician. Police conjecture that his death may be somehow connected to the story he was investigating. Meanwhile, in a second-floor room of the Holiday Plaza, a motel on Holiday Drive, police have found the body of a young woman. Reporter Roger Morgan is live on the scene. Roger?"

Onto the screen flashed Freddie's mother's motel with the leaning palm tree out front. A blond reporter stood in the glare of the TV lights, looking straight into the camera.

But Susan didn't get to hear what Roger had to say because her phone started ringing just as he opened his mouth. When she picked it up, she heard Freddie's breathless voice on the other end of the line.

"Susan? Susan, you'll never guess what—"

"There's a body," Susan said. "Right?"

"Right," Freddie replied. She started to say something, swallowed loudly, and tried again. "Some girl in 2E. They're taking her out on a stretcher." She paused. "I mean, they're taking her out *now*. Not last night. Tonight. Right this minute. The cop in the hall says she was found just a little while ago."

Susan cleared her throat. "If you'll turn on the TV, you can see the whole story."

"Yeah, but we've already seen the whole story. Only we saw it *last* night."

"I know," Susan said, shaking her head to clear it. "It's crazy. I don't get it either."

There was noise on the other end of the line, then Freddie's voice. "I'll talk to you later," she said hurriedly. "Some guy wants to interview me."

Susan put down the phone and turned back to the television.

"The name of the young woman is being withheld until the family has been notified," Roger Morgan was saying. "We'll have more on both these stories as the details come in. We'll be right back after this commercial break." The camera pulled back and a soft-drink commercial came on. Susan turned down the sound.

"I guess they're not going to put in the stuff about the throat," Mack said. "Probably a good idea. People might start looking over their shoulders."

"Throat?" Susan asked. Her voice felt strangled.

"Yeah." Mack frowned. "Like she'd been bit by a snake or something." He looked at her, half-teasing. "Down at the station we've been joking that it looked suspiciously like a vampire bite. You sure you want to stay here by yourself tonight, with

66

vampires on the loose?" Mack asked, his voice sounding like Dracula's.

"I think I'll risk it," Susan said. "But thanks for your concern."

She thought for a moment, then turned to face her brother. "The grave on the beach. Drew Morris's grave. You're sure it was found *today?*"

Mack gave her a puzzled look. "Yeah. That's what I said. Earlier this evening. I was in the station when the call came in. Why do you ask?"

"I think it's just a case of déjà vu," Susan replied. "And it's freaking me out a little."

Mack looked around. "You sure you're not going to be lonesome out here by yourself, Susan? How about if I lend you a couple of kids? I can guarantee the vampires or whatever it is that goes bump in the night won't come around with those boys here. Better than garlic or holy water."

Susan managed a smile. "I think I can handle a few vampires," she said, turning the set off. "But give the boys a hug for me, will you? Tell Betty I'll take them to the beach next week."

Mack drained the last of his iced tea, put his hat back on his head, pushed his feet back into his shoes, and stood up. "Yeah, sure," he said, stretching wearily. "Boy, do I hate the first day back after vacation."

Susan got up too. "Mack," she said, "this Drew Morris guy—do you know anything about him?"

"Nothing that wasn't on TV."

"If you find out anything else, will you please tell me?" Susan asked urgently.

"Yeah, I guess." Mack gave her a look. "Any particular reason?"

For a minute Susan was tempted to tell him. Then she stopped herself. Mack was a hardheaded, practical cop who believed in what you could see, taste, touch, hear, and smell. "Just the facts, ma'am," he liked to say, "just the facts." He'd never believe her. He'd think she was going nuts. Susan pulled in her breath. She had a hard time believing, herself. If Freddie hadn't been here with her last night and seen Drew Morris, Susan would have thought she must have dreamed the whole thing.

"No," she said with a little sigh. "No reason. I'm curious, I guess."

"I'll see what I can dig up," Mack said. "Oops. Sorry about the pun." He was on his way to the door when the lights suddenly flickered.

"That happened last night, too," Susan said. "And the night before."

"Guess I need to check the breaker box," Mack said.

"I'd appreciate that," Susan said. "Thanks for stopping by."

"Don't forget," Mack said, one hand on the knob. "You can have the kids anytime you want them."

"Thanks for the generous offer," Susan said, smiling a little. "Good night."

While Mack clomped noisily down the stairs, Susan closed the door behind him and leaned heavily against it. For a minute she closed her eyes. The whole thing was absolutely preposterous. Crazy. Unbelievable. Drew Morris, reporting on the finding of his own body. Drew Morris, standing beside his own grave, fixing her with the compelling gaze that seemed to speak to her alone.

Susan opened her eyes. The lights flickered again, then went off. As Susan stood wondering whether Mack had shut off the power, the television screen began to glow, as if it had its own independent energy source. As she watched, a face filled the screen.

It was the face of Drew Morris.

Seven

Susan dropped limply into the chair and closed her eyes. There had to be some rational explanation. Maybe she hadn't turned the set off. Maybe the station was making a tribute to the dead newsman. Maybe his picture was on the screen as a memorial. Yes, that was it. That's what had happened. She hadn't actually turned the set off, and when she opened her eyes, the memorial tribute would be over. They'd be showing a sports clip or a commercial or something.

But when Susan opened her eyes, Drew Morris's picture was still there. It obviously wasn't part of a news story. Drew Morris didn't have the combed, collected, in-charge look of a TV journalist. He looked gaunt and disheveled, and the dark shadow of a beard crossed his face. Under the shadow his skin was deathly pale, his gray-green eyes were wide and had an oddly fixed look. Then his lips began to move. Susan had the inescapable feeling that he was saying something to *her*.

She reached for the volume control, and as she did, she saw the power was still off. Her mouth suddenly went dry. Her hand was shaking so badly she could hardly control it.

"—know this sounds idiotic," Drew Morris was saying as Susan turned up the volume. "If I were watching my face on the screen, I'd think the whole thing was crazy too. Or *I* was crazy. Or both." He stopped for a moment as if he were struggling with the words. "I have to deliver a message to somebody named Susan. I can't see you or hear you, Susan, but I have the feeling that you're out there, watching. I hope you're watching." He stopped and rubbed the stubble on his chin. "I really hope you're watching," he said wearily. "Susan, wherever you are, whoever you are, you're in danger. You and your friends. You guys are next."

Susan found herself on her hands and knees, her face inches from the screen. Her breath caught in her throat. "What?" she cried. "What are you talking about?" Then she bit off the words and pulled back. "What am I doing?" Susan said out loud to herself. "This is dumb. I'm talking to a TV set! A TV set that isn't even turned on!"

Drew Morris turned his head, almost as if he were listening. "I know you're out there, Susan. I have the feeling that you believe, even though you don't want to. But you have to listen to me. If you're going to get through this, I mean get through this *alive*, you've got to believe." He closed his eyes for a moment and the screen flickered.

"Believe?" Susan asked hoarsely. "Believe what? That you're dead? That you're alive? That you're talking to me this way?" She reached for the power switch and punched it. "I'll show you how much I believe," she said viciously.

Drew Morris's face remained on the screen, unchanged, even though the power indicator was glowing. "There's a force in your life, Susan," he said, "and you can't control it."

"A force?" Susan cried, feeling half-hysterical. "What I've got is a *television* I can't control!" She hit the power switch again, turning it off.

"—dangerous force," he continued. "A powerful energy that can destroy you completely. I don't fully understand this, either. If I did, I'd tell you more. I want to help you."

"Help me what?" Susan cried.

He didn't hear her. He was smiling grimly, a tortured twist to his mouth. His chuckle had a harsh, grating sound.

73

"Here I am, a newsman with the biggest story of the century, and I can't seem to get the facts straight. I can't . . . *remember*. Everything that's happened to me in the last few weeks is fuzzy, like I'm seeing it through a fog. There was a girl. A girl named Sara. Sara Robertson, I think. She's important, but I can't remember how. And there's other important stuff, things I can't remember at all. I just know they happened. Me dying, for instance."

His hand went to his throat as if he were feeling for something. Then his voice dropped to a gritty, breaking whisper, filled with pain.

"I know I must sound like a lunatic to you, Susan. I'm dead, and I don't know how I died. I've tried to remember, but I can't. All I know is that I died, and somebody stuck my body in a grave on a beach. But if I can't remember anything about the past, I can see a little way into the future. I can see enough to know that you're in danger, you and Freddie and—"

"Freddie?" Susan whispered, the cold fear washing over her. "How do you know—"

But the image of Drew Morris's face had distorted, and the television screen was filled with white snow. An instant later, it went dark. Susan was staring at the dead screen, listening to her heart pound, when the phone rang.

For a moment Susan thought she wouldn't answer it. She'd just let it ring. But then she felt herself getting up, saw her hand reaching for it, heard the tiny sound coming from her throat. She cleared it, and her voice, apprehensive and shaky, said hello.

"The cops just left," Freddie said excitedly.

"What?" Susan asked, not quite connecting.

"The police," Freddie replied. "The TV crews too. They took a bunch of pictures of the building and the motel room and stuff, and they all left. But this reporter was hanging around and I talked to him and—"

Susan's heart thumped heavily in her chest. "What reporter?" she broke in harshly. "What was his name?"

"His name?" Freddie asked. "Oh. Roger something. Morgan, I think. Roger Morgan. A real cute blond. He's the one who did the live report tonight. I watched him do it."

"Oh," Susan said tonelessly. Her fingers were clutching the receiver so hard they hurt.

"Yeah. And listen to this, Suz. Roger says there wasn't anything about a girl's body on last night's news. He says we were dreaming. Or nuts. He says they didn't run any story about a grave on the beach, either. Until tonight, that is." She paused. "That's what you were asking me about the other day, isn't it?"

"Yes," Susan said. She took a breath. She wanted to laugh, but she didn't dare let herself. If she did, she wouldn't be able to stop. The whole thing was crazy, insane. They'd both seen Drew Morris on TV last night. She'd seen his first story, about the grave. She'd seen him tonight, too, with the TV set turned *off*.

"There's something more," Freddie was saying. "This guy, Roger, he says there's something weird about the girl's body. Her throat's got some kind of funny marks on it. Like puncture wounds or something. I wonder if she was on drugs. In the neck, though? Ugh."

Susan thought for a minute. "Freddie, did the reporter tell you the girl's name?"

Freddie paused. "Yeah, he did. Now, let's see, it was . . . I'm not sure I—"

"Sara?" Susan asked.

Freddie sounded surprised. "Yeah, that's it. Sara. Sara Roberts or Robertson or something like that. How'd you know?"

"Lucky guess."

Freddie gave a skeptical laugh. "You picked it out of the air, right? Roger said she was from somewhere up in North Texas. She came down here a couple of weeks ago. She'd only been in the motel for the last three days, Mom said. But apparently they're not putting any of that stuff out until they notify the family, since she was so young." She paused. "So are you going to tell me how you knew?"

Susan tried to swallow the knot of fear that was tightening in her throat. *Sara Robertson. A girl named Sara. She's important, but I don't remember how.*

"I can't tell you right now, Fred," Susan said. "Listen, I'll see you at work tomorrow. Okay?"

Freddie's voice was urgent. "Susan, are you all right? You sound kind of funny. Do you want me to come over?"

"No," Susan said. "Thanks. See you tomorrow." She put the receiver down and turned to stare at the silent television screen. After a while she checked the lock on the back door, pulled out the sleeper-couch, and went to bed. A half hour later she got up and pulled the plug on the television set.

It was after three before she finally fell asleep.

After she hung up the phone, Freddie puzzled for a few minutes over the strange case of the girl in 2E. But she couldn't really concentrate on anything but Flint and the Brothers, and whether she was actually going to be able to sing with them. Oh, she had the job—somehow she'd managed to impress Flint enough to get hired. And she'd done some things with her voice under the spell of the music that had surprised her. Amazed her, really. But she still wasn't sure that she could actually sing the kind of music they played, and she was really worried about the lyrics. If she couldn't remember them long enough to practice them, how would she ever remember them onstage? When her mom turned the office over to the night clerk and came upstairs at midnight, Freddie was sitting at the piano, anxiously one-fingering her way through a piece of music Flint had handed her after the audition—*minus* the lyrics.

Freddie felt better when she went over to the Brothers' house the next night after work. It was her first practice session with the group. The guys, including Brad, were already into a number when she got there. She walked quietly into the old front parlor and sat cross-legged on the floor in the corner, her back to the wall.

She felt better because she had decided something important. The trouble the last time was that she got too deep into the music. The secret was in staying detached. Tonight she'd think while she sang, rather than simply feel her way through. If she could concentrate on technique, she'd be able to figure out what it was that gave the music its vitality.

But as she sat there, thinking became harder and harder. How could she concentrate on technique when there didn't seem to be anything to concentrate on? These guys had mastered their instruments and their sound. They worked together perfectly, as if they were reading each other's minds. All five Brothers, including Brad, stood there with their instruments, wearing dark glasses and playing calmly, easily, *perfectly*, the instruments blending together in a rich, full sound that surged with power and energy. She felt herself being swept up by the sound, pulled by it into some dark place that was far away and somehow not quite . . . safe.

For a while she struggled to stay outside the music. But it was no use. It was like the time she got caught in the undertow at the beach, trying to fight the water and knowing in her heart she couldn't win. Resisting had taken all her energy, had exhausted her. If it hadn't been for Susan, who had seen that she was in trouble and come to her rescue, she would have drowned. But no one was here to rescue her this time. Freddie would have to surrender.

The number ended. Flint smiled at her. "Ah," he said, in his accented English, "I am glad to see you are *listening*. Perhaps now you will struggle less against the music?" He gestured with a commanding motion toward an empty stool beside him. "Come now and sing with us, Frederica."

Without knowing exactly how she got there, Freddie found herself sitting on the stool. Flint leaned toward her, the single light in the room glinting off his dark glasses. He dropped a soft kiss on her cheek.

"Now," he said, "let us do the song Frederica sang with us last night, at the audition."

"I need a lyric sheet," Freddie said. "I don't remember the words."

Flint put his hand on her arm. "The lyrics will come to you when you give yourself to the music," he said softly. "Do not try to learn it with your mind—feel it with your heart."

"But how can I sing it without learning it?"

Flint smiled slightly. "Let the music teach you," he said.

Freddie found herself too tired to argue with him, almost too tired to sing. As the Brothers began to play, she tried to think where she was supposed to come in, tried to remember the words. But it was too hard. She missed her first cue. Then she missed her second. Then, when she'd given up completely, it all suddenly came together: the cue, the lyrics, the power. Her voice was deep and full—majestic, even. As the rhythms and sounds filled her soul, she welcomed them. The music was as cool and sweet as the spring tides, as profound as the farthest depths of the ocean, and as inviting as the softest whisper. And the words made sense. They made perfect sense.

The group practiced for what seemed like hours, but might have been only a few moments. Freddie didn't know and didn't care. Her anxiety had gone, and she was left feeling calm, soft, open.

She could have sung all night. She actually hoped she would. Then with a slight hand movement, Flint stopped the band.

"I think," he said, "we will be ready to open on Saturday. Do you agree?" The Brothers all nodded. They put down their instruments, as if on a signal, and left the room.

Flint took off his glasses and looked intently at Freddie. His dark eyes were warm, appreciative, full of admiration for the work she had done tonight. Freddie smiled at him.

"You are beginning to feel the music," he said. "You are now inviting it inside of you. It is so?"

"Yes," Freddie said.

"And you are enjoying it?"

"Yes," Freddie repeated dreamily. "It feels good. It feels right." She rested her head on Flint's shoulder.

It was late, and she was tired. Which was entirely too bad, because the Brothers had conveniently left them alone. And Flint was so attractive, so powerfully, irresistibly attractive. The room seemed to fill with a darkening haze. The guys must be playing somewhere at the back of the house, she thought dimly. She could hear the music, faint and sweet and alluring, as Flint leaned toward her and kissed her softly.

Freddie wasn't sure what time it was when she got home. The next morning she slept through the alarm. She was nearly an hour late getting to work.

Angie sat down angrily across the table from Brad. She hadn't seen him since he'd started playing with the Blood Brothers. When she took him his pizza ten minutes ago, he'd surprised her with some startling news—news that made her go numb. Unfortunately, the place had been so busy, she couldn't talk to him then. Now she was breaking all kinds of rules by sitting down, even though she was on her break. Gwen didn't like her employees to sit with the customers, especially when the dining room was full. But tonight Angie didn't care. She was mad and had to find out what was going on.

"What exactly are you trying to tell me?" she asked, trying to keep her voice level. She wished Brad would take off those sunglasses he was wearing. She couldn't see his eyes. She couldn't see what he was thinking.

Brad pushed his pizza away, even though he'd barely touched it. "Like I said," he said flatly. "I've moved in with the Brothers. I just finished hauling my stuff over there. It's a big old house. Plenty of room for everybody. And this way we can practice at any time."

Angie stared at him. "But I thought . . ." There was a hard lump in her throat, and she had to blink to keep the tears back. Before he started playing with the band, Angela thought that he might be ready to make a commitment sometime soon. And he had. But the commitment he made was to the band, not to her.

Brad leaned across the table. "Angie, this doesn't mean I don't want to live with you. You mean a lot to me. I still love you. I want you near me always. Forever." He looked deep into her eyes and kissed her softly on her lips. "That's why I want you to move in with me."

Angie's eyes widened. "But you already moved in with someone else. Four someone elses."

"Yeah. So? As I say, it's a big house. Flint would let us have our own private room. There's a bathroom at the end of the hall, and a huge kitchen. If we live there, we can save a lot of money and be together all the time. And you can have people over to visit—Nita can stay with us whenever you want. There really is a lot of room."

Angie looked down at her hands. "Do you think you're ready for something like this?" she whispered. "I mean . . ."

"You mean, am I ready for a commitment?" Brad's lips curled up in a smile. "You know me, babe. I'm not into commitments in a major way. But if it'll make you happy . . . I mean, there's nobody else, I swear. I'm not interested in girls, plural. Just you." He took her hands in his. "Just us."

"But I can't move in with . . . a bunch of guys," Angie replied, flustered. "It wouldn't be . . . my folks would be really upset." She shuddered, imagining how strange it would be. To move in with Brad, whom she loved, would be a big enough deal. But to move in with the whole band?

Brad scowled. "When are you going to stop thinking about your parents and start thinking about us? You're not a kid anymore, Angie. You're a woman. It's time you grew up and stopped taking orders from home." He leaned back. "It would be good for you to live with my music for a while, too. That way you'll know how you really feel about me."

"Live with your music?" Angie asked. She searched Brad's face. There was something different about him. It wasn't just that he hadn't even touched his food. She couldn't be sure what it was, especially because she couldn't see his eyes. He seemed tired and impatient, not his usual easygoing self.

"Yeah, live with the music," Brad repeated. "You're interested in what I'm doing, aren't you?"

Angie nodded wordlessly.

"Well, then, you ought to get into the music with me. You can't love me if you can't love my music." Brad pouted a little when he said it.

Brad had played with other groups since they'd been going together, and he'd never insisted that she get involved with his music. As a matter of fact, he used to like it that the music was separate. It was a kind of private place that belonged only to him. And she had always been more than happy to stay out of this part of his life.

As if he had read her mind, Brad said, "Yeah, I know. You don't like the stuff I'm into. And I've always kind of kept it apart from what was ours together. But I see now that that was wrong. If we're going to be together—I mean, *really* together—there can't be anything between us. We've got to share everything. The music, especially."

Angie got a warm feeling inside her for the first time since they started this argument. *We've got to share everything.* Yes, that was right. Two people who loved one another ought to share. But she still didn't see how she could compromise her own values and upset her father.

Before Angie could even respond, Brad pushed back abruptly from the table. "Come on," he said, jerking his head. "Walk me to the car." He held out his hand to her.

Angie looked at her watch, then looked back toward Gwen's office. "I've only got five minutes left on my break," she said.

"Come on, then," Brad said roughly, thrusting his hand into his pocket. "We're wasting time."

Angie got up and followed him outside into the early-evening dark. They walked around the corner to a quiet street where the car was parked. He opened the door and motioned her in with a quick, impatient gesture. He got in too and pulled her against him.

"Hey," he said, when she pushed away. "What's the matter? We haven't seen one another for three days, remember?" He kissed her, hard.

Angie shivered. When she looked up at him, she saw only herself, reflected in the dark glasses. "What is it, Brad?" she whispered.

"What's what?"

"You. You're different. What is it? Is it the guys you're playing with?"

"I don't know what you're talking about," Brad said. He put his fingers under her chin and tilted it up. "I'm me," he said softly, "the guy who's crazy for you. You're the one who's acting funny." His mouth was on hers again, then on her face, her throat.

Angie pulled in her breath. The way he was kissing her, it *was* different. More urgent, more demanding. It was a little scary, but also pretty exciting. "Not now, Brad," she managed breathlessly, at last. "How about later tonight, huh? After I get off work. I've got to get back now, or Gwen will have my head."

Brad sat back against the seat. "I can't later," he said. "We're practicing tonight. The opening's on Saturday. You're coming, right?" It wasn't so much a question as a command.

Angie nodded slowly. She wasn't exactly looking forward to an entire evening of loud rock in some dark club. But she had to show Brad she supported him. And, of course, it was Freddie's opening night too. She wanted to hear Freddie sing.

"Susan and I are coming together," she said. "Juanita's coming too."

Brad grinned. "Nita? Great! I'll introduce her to Russel, our drummer. I bet he'd go for her."

Angie frowned. She wasn't sure she wanted her sister to start hanging around with Russel. She was only sixteen.

But she didn't say that to Brad. She just said, "We'll see," and kissed him quickly.

"About moving in—?"

"Let's talk about it later," Angie said, and got out of the car. As she walked back to the Pizzeria, though, she was sorry she'd said that. Brad might think she was actually considering it as a real option.

Still, the thought wouldn't leave her. It would be wonderful to be able to spend all their free time together. And her insides went soft at the thought that he loved her enough to want her to share his music. He was different from the last time they'd been together, there was no denying that. There was a new kind of energy in him, in his kisses, that made her pulse race.

Yes, it was scary.

At the same time, it was wildly exciting.

Eight

It was nearly nine on Saturday night, and the hot, humid darkness of a Galveston summer night blanketed the city. Susan stopped her car—the secondhand blue Honda she'd bought with last summer's paychecks—in front of the small frame house where Angie lived. They were headed to Dark of the Moon, where Freddie and Brad were having their big debut with the Blood Brothers.

Susan tapped the horn twice. As she waited for Angie and Nita to come out of the house, she wondered how Freddie was feeling. Susan had called the motel earlier to wish her luck, but Mrs. Gardner reported that Freddie had already gone over to the Brothers' house. She sounded irritated.

"I've hardly seen Freddie since she got involved with that new band," she said. She had never been very enthusiastic about her daughter's singing, and she seemed even less so now. "And from what I've seen," she added with a motherly sniff, "I don't like it very much at all. Whatever that group is doing to her, it's not good."

Talking about Freddie behind her back made Susan uncomfortable, but she had to admit that she agreed with Freddie's mom. Since Freddie had started practicing with the Brothers, she'd become remote and out of touch with the people around her, almost as if she weren't there at all. She'd made dozens of mistakes at work, and Susan had done a lot of covering up. Thinking about it, she wondered whether it was the late nights or Freddie's romance with Flint that was making the difference in her. Whatever it was, Freddie was certainly acting dopey and confused. When she'd shortchanged the second customer in a row, Susan had mentioned it to her. Freddie just shrugged and smiled in a lazy way that accused *Susan* of acting strange.

Susan made a grim face. Freddie might be right about that—Susan *had* been acting strange lately. But Susan didn't have to look farther than her own living room for the cause. She hadn't reconnected her television set. That had been a gesture that said, plain as day, I don't want to hear from you, Drew Morris. She hadn't been bothered by his voice or his face since.

But that didn't mean she hadn't thought about him and his bizarre message. And the eerie mystery that continued to surround the grave on the beach. And the death of Sara Robertson, the girl from Dallas. It frightened her to think about it, but the image of Drew Morris—his intense face, his commanding eyes—stayed with her, even when she tried to shut him out of her mind.

As much as Susan tried to escape the reality of these horrors, she couldn't escape Mack, who apparently thought it was his duty to keep her up-to-date on the developments in both murder cases. He especially seemed to get a kick out of giving her the coroner's reports. Drew Morris had died of a heart attack. That seemed strange in somebody so young, but apparently there was a history of heart disease in his family. So the cause of death was pretty straightforward. The only mystery now was how his body had come to lie in a shallow grave on the beach behind the SeaWall Condominium.

Sara Robertson had died of something called pernicious anemia, something about a low red blood cell count—although there hadn't been any indication that she'd been suffering from any illness. The coroner's office couldn't account for the strange puncture marks on her neck, but they'd ruled out drug use. Neither case was high priority with the cops, according to Mack, since both victims had died of natural causes. They weren't murdered.

"You mean, it's okay for somebody to bury a body on the beach?" Susan had asked.

Mack shrugged. "Not exactly. But whoever did it didn't leave a card. Besides, we've run out of leads."

So there it was. Two deaths, two mysteries. And a television set with a mind of its own telling her that she and her friends were in danger. It was no wonder she'd been acting as if she'd had something on her mind lately.

"Hi," Angie said brightly. She plopped down in the front seat as Nita got into the back. Both sisters looked pretty in crisp, summery dresses and strappy sandals, their long hair loose and flowing. Susan had opted for something more casual, a short denim skirt, simple yellow top, yellow sandals.

Angie's Aunt Carlota had come out of the house with the girls to see them off. She paused by the car. "You know," she added a little uneasily, "I don't think I like the idea of you girls going to a place called Dark of the Moon. All kinds of strange things can happen in the dark of the moon. It is the witching hour of the night: a time for evil."

"Oh, don't be silly, Aunt Carlota." Nita giggled. "You think of things like that because you're a witch. It's a theme club for teens. It's completely innocent. The name doesn't mean anything."

"A name like that means *something*," Aunt Carlota said. "You girls should be careful."

"We will," Susan promised. She liked Angie's aunt, even though she didn't quite believe the superstitions and the old magic she practiced. But Aunt Carlota did have a great many believers around Galveston. For a moment Susan wondered if Aunt Carlota could maybe use her magic to find out who had dug the grave on the beach, or how the weird marks had come to be on Sara Robertson's neck. Perhaps she could even explain the face on Susan's TV screen.

But this wasn't the time to ask. Besides, if she told her about Drew Morris's face on the television screen, Aunt Carlota would probably insist on coming over to exorcise the evil spirits from her apartment. Susan wasn't ready for that. She said good-bye and backed out of the driveway.

Susan was beginning to feel better about the night ahead of her. At the very least it would help her to forget about Drew Morris.

Dark of the Moon was packed by the time Susan, Angie, and Juanita showed up. The band wasn't on yet, but some people were dancing to the jukebox. Susan was afraid they wouldn't be able to find seats, until Angie found the table Brad had reserved for her. Looking around, Susan was amazed at the number of people who had shown up. They'd probably been drawn to the theme, Susan decided, since they probably never heard of the band.

Dark of the Moon. The club certainly lived up to its name, Susan thought. Angie's aunt would probably have dragged them out of there in an instant. Ghoulish caped figures with dead-white faces and staring eyes took money at the door. Bats hung from the ceiling, and skeletons glowed purple under black lights. Open coffins stood in the corners, covered with cobwebs. The waiters wore black T-shirts and black jeans, white face makeup, and blood-red lipstick.

But Susan didn't think the theme was hip or cool. The bats made her shudder, and she had the feeling that the ghouls were watching her with their red-rimmed eyes. The whole atmosphere was entirely too creepy for her liking, and it was making her uncomfortable.

At nine thirty someone switched off the jukebox, and the band came out wearing all black, with dark sunglasses, as usual. Flint gave a brief welcome to the club and introduced the members of the band. Susan had to admit that his low, accented voice had an intriguing quality. She glanced over at Nita and Angie. Nita was almost hypnotized by Flint and by what he was saying. Angie, of course, was staring at Brad. Susan glanced at Freddie, standing behind Flint. She was wearing a short, tight, sleeveless black dress, cut very low in the back. Freddie's attention, like that of practically every other girl in the club, was riveted on Flint.

When the band began their first number, and Freddie began to sing, Susan understood immediately why she had called the music seductive. Susan found it captivating, mesmerizing. It was as eerily hypnotic as Flint's voice had been. But it wasn't just the music—it was the lyrics, too. They were slippery and hard to catch. The few phrases she did understand made her feel unaccountably uneasy. She was glad that they vanished from her head as soon as she heard them, like words heard in a dream.

With an effort Susan pulled herself away from the music and looked around at the rapt faces. Nobody was moving. The few people who had been on the dance floor were now sitting down and listening. Almost everybody seemed to be captivated by the music. Those who weren't, like her, were glancing around uncomfortably. A few were leaving.

By the end of the set, Susan was distressed and fidgety. She would have left, but her friends showed no sign of moving, and she couldn't leave them there. As the houselights brightened, the Brothers came over to their table and sat down.

Susan tried to make conversation with Freddie, telling her how well she sang and how great she looked and how much fun the club was, but she might as well have been talking to a wall. Freddie was moody and silent. She didn't even look at Susan as she spoke—all her attention was focused on Flint. In fact, nobody seemed to want to talk very much. Angie and Brad were dancing, but the others just seemed to want to sit and listen to the jukebox play the Brothers' music.

After a little while Bishop asked Susan to dance with him. Feeling bored and sleepy and hoping that some physical movement might break the spell, Susan agreed.

On the floor Susan felt heavy and languid, as if she were half-asleep. The lights were dizzying. Mirrored balls hung from the ceiling, catching the colored lights and sprinkling them onto the dance floor. The fingers of color reached into her, making her feel light-headed and giddy, and she stumbled.

"You're fighting it," Bishop whispered in her ear, tightening his arms around her. "Go with the music. Let it take you."

Susan knew that Bishop was right. That's what you did when you danced, you went with the music, you let it take you. But she didn't *want* this music to take her. It was totally irrational, she knew, but she felt somehow threatened by the group's music. It was almost as if the music itself wanted something from her, something she was unwilling to give.

She felt threatened by Bishop in the same way, Susan realized. He had a strange effect on her. Susan had dated before, and she'd even thought she was in love once or twice. This was different. She was breathless, and her pulse was beating fast and hot in her throat. In Bishop's arms her body felt fluid, wanting to move in a different way. The feeling frightened her. She was trembling and she held herself tightly, making an effort to conceal how she felt.

"You don't have to be so stiff, you know," Bishop said, looking down at her. His glance was unreadable behind his glasses, but his lips were curved in a slight smile. "Loosen up, Susan. I'm not going to hurt you. I want you to have fun, that's all." He held her closer then, forcing her body to move with his.

And then, suddenly, she was dancing, easily and lightly, without intention, without thought. It was as if she were in a trance, in a dream. Everything else disappeared, too, the lights, the room—it was just she and Bishop and the sweet music that wrapped them up and pulled them in.

The next thing she knew, she was sitting at the table again, breathless, flushed, her pulse racing.

"Did you and Bishop have a good dance?" Angie asked.

"What?" Susan asked. Her head felt thick and fuzzy, and somewhere deep inside her there was an unmistakable cold fear.

Nita giggled. "You were really *gone*," she said. "Russel and I danced by and said hi, and you didn't even notice. Gee, I wonder what they're putting into those drinks."

Angie leaned closer. "Are you okay, Susan?" she asked. "You look kind of . . . strange."

"I have a headache," Susan said, closing her eyes. The fear and apprehension in her middle grew tighter, like a knot. "I guess it's the music."

It was the music, and more. It was Bishop, and the way he had held her, and the club, and . . .

Susan's headache began to pound.

The second set had ended, and Angie was waiting for Brad to come back to the table. She couldn't believe how much she was enjoying the music, the club, the people. There had been a wonderful misty quality to the evening, as if she'd been wrapped in a silvery, dreamlike fog filled with soft sparkles of pastel light that exploded like Roman candles in the velvety darkness. She couldn't remember ever feeling this wonderful before.

It was funny, too. She hadn't looked forward to the music, yet that was what she had loved most tonight. She had been fascinated by its strange, eerie sound, the way it reached out for her and pulled her into its deep rhythms, making her want to relax and let it flow through her, like a warm, honey-sweet river. The music and the lyrics opened a part of her that she hadn't known existed. She loved listening to the words Freddie sang, words that seemed to speak to her inner being. She just wished she could remember them when the song was over.

Most of all, she loved watching Brad play. For her he was the star of the entire show. Several times during the set he'd looked up and smiled at her—a slow, sexy smile that made her heart pound. Yes, they *could* share the music, Angie decided, the way he wanted them to. She could come to the club every night and listen. Maybe she could even—

She pushed the thought away. No, she couldn't

move in with him. It was out of the question. But watching Brad, she felt the temptation. Swaying dreamily to the music, she couldn't help thinking how wonderful it would be if . . .

When the set was over, Susan leaned across the table. "Angie, I've got a ferocious headache. Are you ready to go?"

"What did you say?" Angie asked. The melody of the last song was still echoing in her head, and she felt so dreamy that it required an effort of will to focus her attention on what Susan was saying. If she didn't know better, she'd almost think she was drunk. But that was silly. This was a teen club and there was no alcohol. No, if she was feeling hazy, it was the wonderful effect of the music.

"I said," Susan repeated, "that I have a headache. Are you and Nita ready to go?"

Angie looked across the floor. Brad would be here in a moment, and they were going to dance again. The jukebox was playing one of the Brothers' songs, and Nita was dancing with Russel. They really seemed to be hitting it off. When Brad had mentioned that he wanted to introduce them, Angie hadn't thought it was a good idea. Now, though, it seemed perfect. It seemed to round everything out: she and Brad, Nita and Russel, Freddie and Flint. Now, if only Susan would stop being such a spoilsport and give Bishop a chance—

"Where's Bishop?" she asked. It was hard to make her mouth form the words.

"I don't know," Susan replied. "My head hurts. I can't think about anything right now, including Bishop." She reached for her purse. *Especially Bishop,* she added silently to herself. "I've got to get out of here, Angie. Are you coming with me, or are you going to wait for Brad?"

Angie smiled. "Brad will take me home," she said. "We'll go to the Brothers' house first so I can see the place. Freddie will come too." She put her hand on Susan's arm. "Why don't you come with us, Susan? We can have a party." She pointed across the crowded room. "Look, there's Bishop. I'm sure he'll ask you to dance with him again. Why don't you stay?"

Susan didn't look at Bishop. She leaned toward Angie. "Are you all right, Angie? You're not acting like yourself."

Angie tossed her hair back over her shoulder with a wicked laugh. Oh, Susan, always so smart, always thinking she had the right answer. But tonight she was wrong. Tonight, for the first time in her life, Angie felt she was being her real, true self. Ever since they'd started going together, Brad had accused her of being prudish and old-fashioned. But the real Angie wasn't like that at all, and the Brothers' music had helped her to escape.

She was the Angie who understood that whatever feels good *is* good. The Angie who knew how to let herself go, knew how to have fun. And tonight she was going to show Brad how much fun the *real* Angie could be.

"I'm fine," Angie said. The Brothers' music on the jukebox grew louder, and she smiled.

Susan got up. "How about Nita?"

"She's fine too."

"Well, good night," Susan said. She stood for a moment, as if she were hoping that Angie would change her mind. Then, abruptly, she was gone.

Brad came over. "What's the matter with Susan?" he asked gruffly. "Doesn't she like the music?"

Angie kept smiling. "She just thinks too much. She'll be okay."

Brad pulled her up and she went into his arms. "Let's not worry about Susan," he said into her ear. "Bishop will take care of her."

"That's good," Angie said, pressing herself against him. "Susan needs somebody to take care of her. The way you take care of me."

"Yeah," Brad said. He laughed a little. "That's exactly what she needs."

Angie didn't answer. She wasn't worried about Susan. She wasn't worried about Nita, either. She wasn't thinking of anyone but Brad. And the music. The music that pulsed softly through her with the rhythm of her own blood. The music that was letting her be herself, for the first time in her life.

It was after midnight when Susan got back to her apartment and let herself into the dark living room. She didn't turn the light on. She just sat down on the sofa, across from the silent television screen, and stared into the darkness. The moon, full and round, made a silvery lagoon on the floor.

The fear that she'd felt back at the club was still with her, though it was heavier now, and more real. She hadn't wanted to leave Angie and Nita behind, or Freddie either. A part of her had wanted to insist that they all leave together, that it wasn't safe to stay. That there was some kind of dangerous force that threatened to pull them in, pull them under.

But another part of her, the rational part, knew that she was overreacting. Dark of the Moon was a club with a trendy theme. There was nothing to be afraid of. Besides, Angie and Freddie—even Nita—were old enough to know what they were doing.

Susan looked down at her hands. If there was nothing to be afraid of, why were her palms sweaty and slick? Why was this terrible feeling of foreboding making her stomach feel queasy? And worst of all, why did she feel, with an absolute, desolate certainty, that she had said good-bye to Freddie and Angie and Brad and Nita for the last time?

You're in danger, you and your friends. You're next.

The voice, uninvited, came from the back of her mind. It came with a loud clarity that made her sit up straight and pull in her breath.

I want to help.

"Then help," Susan whispered out loud. "What is this thing I'm so afraid of?"

You believe—but you don't want to believe. If you're going to get through to me, you've got to believe.

For a minute Susan sat still. Then, moving deliberately, she got up and plugged in the television set. She sat down again and folded her hands in her lap, waiting.

Feeling sillier and sillier by the minute.

You goose, the rational part of herself said in a dry, sarcastic tone. *What do you think you're doing? Waiting for someone to commune with you through the TV? Have you totally lost your mind?*

There was a soft knock on the door. Susan started violently, cold fear lancing through her. Who could it be at this hour of the night?

She swallowed. It wasn't that late, really. The knock was probably Mack or Betty. They'd heard her drive up and wanted her to baby-sit tomorrow. Or maybe it was Angie, or Freddie. Maybe they'd changed their minds about going to the Brothers' house and decided to stop by.

Without turning on the light, Susan got up and went to the door. There wasn't anything to be afraid of, but there wasn't any point in taking risks, either. She left the chain on and opened the door cautiously, just a crack.

"Who is it?" she asked.

"Hey, Susan," a soft voice said. "Why don't you invite me in?"

Nine

Susan's breath caught in her throat. "Bishop?"

"Yeah. You left without saying good night."

Susan leaned against the wall next to the door, her knees suddenly weak. She was feeling the way she had felt when she and Bishop danced. "I . . . I had a headache," she whispered.

"That's too bad," Bishop said. "It was probably the lights. They kind of get to me, too. That's why I wear dark glasses when I play." He paused. "Listen, would you mind asking me in for a minute or two? I promise not to stay too long. I want to talk, that's all. We didn't really get to talk tonight, and there's so much to say."

He was right, Susan thought dimly. There *was* so much to say, so much—She saw her hand on the chain, felt her shoulder muscles tense to open the door. Then she stopped and summoned her strength to resist. "I don't think so, Bishop," she heard herself say. "It's late, and I need to—"

"It's not that late," Bishop said. He put his mouth to the crack in the door. "I really liked dancing with you, Susan. I brought a tape. I thought maybe we could dance together, just the two of us. Would you like that?"

Yes, Susan thought, remembering how it had felt to let herself go with the music. *I would like that.*

"Then invite me in," he said, as if he had read her thoughts. His voice was soft and gentle, a whisper. But the command was imperative. "Invite me in, Susan."

Susan felt herself weakening. There was no harm in inviting Bishop to come in for a little while. They could talk and dance. . . .

"Please," he said softly, forcefully.

Susan lifted the chain on the door and opened it. "Come in," she said, stepping back.

Bishop smiled lazily and stepped through the door. He was still wearing his black outfit, but he'd taken off the dark glasses. He looked around the apartment. "Very nice," he said approvingly. "I like it."

"I'll turn on the light," Susan offered, moving toward the lamp. In the corner she noticed that the television screen was glowing softly, as if it were on. She'd probably forgotten to turn the power switch off before she unplugged it. When she'd plugged it in again, it had come on by itself.

Bishop moved swiftly between her and the lamp. "No," he said. He gestured toward the open window, where the moonlight was streaming in, soft and silvery. "It's perfect like this, don't you think?"

Susan was about to object. But suddenly it didn't seem important. Bishop was right—the room was perfect with just the moonlight, her, and him. She smiled to herself, glad he had come. It would be nice to have a talk and to dance a little.

Bishop looked around. "Do you have a tape player?" he asked.

Susan pointed to the bookshelf. Bishop walked over and put the tape on, turning the volume down low. The music—soft and sensual—began to fill the room.

Susan's breath caught, her eyes widened. There was that feeling again, that cold apprehension, deep inside. It made her want to resist, struggle—to put her fingers in her ears and shut out the invasive sounds of the words.

Bishop moved toward her, his arms out. "Dance?" he asked. He was smiling. In the moonlit shadows his eyes were pools of deep, lovely darkness, with tiny dancing lights.

Susan found herself growing breathless. In the

next instant, without meaning to, she was moving toward him, lifting her arms. There was nothing to be afraid of, nothing to struggle against. Looking into his eyes, she could forget her apprehensions, her childish need to resist. Looking into his eyes, she knew she need never be afraid again. She would be one with Bishop and the music and—

Danger.

The single word was so clear and emphatic that Susan was sure it had been spoken out loud. But there were only the two of them in the room. She pulled her eyes away from Bishop's and glanced at the TV. The screen was blank.

"Look at me, Susan," Bishop whispered. He put his fingers on her cheek and gently turned her face toward him.

Suddenly Susan was frightened. No, it was greater than that. A cold terror sliced through her like a knife. If she gave in to Bishop, to the music, *to the dream*, she would be lost. Forever. And she knew it with the utmost certainty.

She closed her eyes. "Help me," she whispered out loud, her words a plea. "Oh, please, *help* me!"

The television set crackled.

"It's okay," Bishop said in a low, crooning voice. His eyes were still fixed on hers. He put his hand on her shoulder. "Let's turn the set off. We don't want to watch TV, anyway, do we?"

"I'll turn the set off," Susan heard herself saying mechanically. "We don't want to watch TV."

But as she moved slowly toward the set, the screen began to brighten, and a picture came on.

The face on the screen was that of Drew Morris.

Angie and Nita got out of Brad's car in front of the Brothers' house.

"This is it," Brad said.

Russel climbed out and shut the car door behind him. "Great place, huh?"

Nita glanced across the street. "You've got to be kidding," she said. She wrinkled her nose. "A cemetery?"

Brad laughed. "Hey, dead people are perfect neighbors. They don't call the cops because of a little noise late at night." He reached for Angie's hand. "Come on. I want to show you something."

Angie cast a look back at her sister. "I can't stay too long," she said. "I don't want to get in trouble for keeping Nita out too late."

"That's fine," Brad said. "But if you ask me, Nita doesn't seem to care if she ever goes home again." Angie looked over and saw Nita was saying something to Russel with a giggle, and he had his arm around her shoulders.

"Where are we going?" Angie asked, as Brad led her into the house and down the front hall, past stacks of big instrument cases. It was a huge old house, dark and shadowy. No wonder the Brothers had come up with such a spooky theme for their club. They'd probably thought of it right here, in this very hall.

"Let's go upstairs," Brad said. "I want to show you my room."

"Really, Brad," Angie said, holding back. "I—" She stopped. *Wait*, she told herself. *That's the old Angie talking.* The *real* Angie wouldn't be afraid to let Brad show her his room, sit down, and talk for a while. Then she'd collect Nita, and Brad could take them both home, long before her father began wondering where they were.

Brad's room was at the end of the upstairs hall. He opened the door and Angie followed him in. He lit a candle.

"Don't you have any lights?" Angie asked.

Brad chuckled. "Sure. But I like the candle. It's more romantic, don't you think?" He gestured around the room. "What do you think of the posters?"

In the flickering light of the candle, the posters had a dark, powerful effect. They were full-size pictures of the Brothers with their instruments.

"Nice, huh?" Brad asked.

Angie nodded.

He followed Angie's gaze as she looked around the room. "See how big this place is? More than enough space for both of us."

"I don't think—" Angie began automatically. Then she stopped.

Brad looked down at her. He'd taken off his dark glasses, and his eyes were a pale blue, glittering in the darkness. "Don't say no," he instructed her. "Say, 'I'll think about it.'"

"I . . . I'll think about it," Angie whispered.

"That's my girl," Brad said. He kissed the dimple in her chin. The hollow of her throat. Her mouth.

Angie clung to him dizzily, trusting his strong, powerful arms to hold her, to keep her from falling. She loved the way Brad was kissing her, the way he was holding her. It was almost perfect. There was only one thing that would make everything even better.

"Brad," she said dreamily, when he had lifted his lips from hers, "could we listen to some of the Brothers' music?"

Brad chuckled. "Yeah," he said. "If that's what you want."

"That's what I want," Angie said softly. "More than anything." She pulled his head down to hers and kissed him again. "Almost anything."

Freddie sat at the table, her chin in her hands. She felt absolutely wrung out, as if she'd just finished running a marathon. It was long after midnight, and the club was empty except

113

for her and Flint. They were alone. At last.

Flint stepped out of the office, locking the door behind him. He came over to the table. Standing behind her, he put his hands on the back of her neck and began to massage gently.

"Are you tired, Frederica?" he asked.

"Yes," Freddie said. "Very. It was a big night. We were a hit, don't you think?"

The truth was, though, that she couldn't remember most of the evening. It was the same way when they practiced. Once she invited the music inside her, she could never recall what happened. It was a very strange sensation. But each time it was easier to give in, to let the music take over. If only she weren't so tired afterward, it would be wonderful.

Flint sat down across from Freddie and took off his glasses. "You were very good, Frederica." He stroked her arm. "You bring a new life to the lyrics."

"Do you think so?" Freddie's arm tingled where he was stroking it.

"I know so," Flint said. He picked up her arm and kissed the inside of her wrist, very gently. "You are one of us. Isn't it so?" He looked at her.

"Yes," Freddie whispered. "Yes, it is so." She shivered as his lips came down on her wrist.

Susan stood staring at Drew's image on the

television screen, feeling the blood drain from her face, the roaring in her ears almost drowning out the music.

"Susan," Bishop said sternly, stepping forward, "we don't want to watch television. We have better things—" He stopped when he saw the face on the screen.

"Hello, Bishop," Drew said.

"*You!*" Bishop hollered. He stepped back, his mouth twisted, ugly. "What are you doing here?"

Susan reached for a chair to steady herself. "You know him?" she whispered incredulously.

Bishop didn't answer. But he didn't need to. Susan could read his feelings in his face. Bishop knew Drew Morris. And he was afraid of him. Mortally afraid.

"Turn off the music, Susan," Drew Morris said gently. "You'll be able to think better with the music off. And Bishop and I can have a little talk."

Susan took a step toward the tape player. Bishop glared at her. "Leave it on," he said.

"No," Susan whispered. She groped her way to the tape player and switched it off. It was like stepping out of a fog bank into clear air.

Bishop thrust her aside roughly and strode to the door. Hand on the knob, he turned. His face was white, his eyes glittered like black diamonds, his jaw clenched.

"Don't think you're going to get away with this," he growled. "Give it up, Morris. You've already lost. You're a dead man."

"Then why are you leaving?" Drew Morris asked. "We need to talk, you know. There's an old misunderstanding we have to clear up."

Bishop's only answer was another savage growl. He walked back to the center of the room to confront the image on the screen. "We don't *need* to talk about anything," Bishop said. "And even if we did, I don't take orders from mortals. Especially dead ones."

"Ah, Bishop," Drew said. "Now I remember your stubbornness. But I, too, plan to stick around. I may be dead, but I am not gone."

With that Bishop turned and strode back to the door. He jerked it open and flew down the stairs. A minute later Susan heard Bishop's car tires spinning on the gravel; then he was gone.

Susan turned back to the television set, half expecting Drew Morris to be gone too. But he was still there. She dropped down on the sofa, her knees so weak she could no longer stand. Her mouth was dry. Her hands were trembling. "Drew?" she whispered. She knew it was crazy to be talking to the television, but no less crazy than what had just happened. Anyway, she had to talk to him. Insane as it was, she *had* to.

"I need to know what's going on," she said in a

low voice. She knotted her fingers together. "You said before that you couldn't remember everything, but I need to know what you know. I need to know what the danger is."

Drew Morris's pale gray-green eyes regarded her seriously. "I was doing a story on runaways," he said slowly. "A girl named Sara"—he paused for a moment, then his face brightened—"Robertson. She was my lead." He closed his eyes for a moment. When he opened them again, he spoke slowly, as if his memories were coming back bit by bit. "When I got onto her, she was a groupie, hanging around with this band in Dallas. Yes, that's how it was. She came down here, and I followed her, hoping to find out why—" He broke off.

"Tell me," Susan urged. "Tell me, Drew."

"Look," he said flatly. "This isn't the kind of thing any rational person would believe. But you *have* to. If you don't believe me, Susan, I can't help you. And you won't be able to help your friends. So before I go any further with this crazy, twisted tale, I need to know that your heart is in the fight. There's a lot of work ahead of you, and I need to be sure of your commitment."

"Tell me," Susan repeated urgently. "*Please.*"

"Sara Robertson came here with the Blood Brothers, the band your friend Bishop plays in. And they got her. I suspect they got other

117

groupies, too—several teens in the Dallas area disappeared while the Brothers were there. But I know they got Sara, because I saw it." He managed a thin chuckle. "They tried to get me too, but I outfoxed them."

Susan stared at him. "What do you mean they tried to get you? And how'd you outfox them?"

"I died first."

"You died first," Susan repeated automatically. Then the true meaning of the words sank in. Her eyes opened wide. "Do you mean they *killed* people? And they tried to kill *you?*" she asked in a shocked whisper.

"Yes. But there's a law, you see, that they can't take what you won't give them. And I'd known about the bad heart for a long while. I knew they were onto me, that I was beginning to know too much. I didn't have much time left, so I checked out before they could get me." Drew chuckled again, wryly. "I'll bet the Brothers don't have many of their victims just up and *die* on them. . . ."

"Wait a minute," Susan said, confused. "What law? *Whose* law?"

"Whoever's running this show. I'm finding out that there's a lot I don't know about the way these things work. I'm learning quickly, though." He was beginning to sound excited. "I'm telling you, Susan, if I could only file a story from here—" He glanced around. "Wherever here is."

Susan cleared her throat. "Sara Robertson," she said, trying to gain control of her voice. "How did she die?"

Drew's mouth twisted. "The Brothers were out for blood."

"You mean they wanted revenge? Why? What did she do to them?"

"Sara? She didn't do anything. It was completely random. I'm telling you, they were simply out for blood."

"Then why—?" She clenched her hands. "Drew, will you please stop talking in circles? What is it about the Brothers that makes them want to kill people?"

"Do you believe?"

"How can I know if I believe," she countered, "if you won't *tell* me!"

Drew looked at her, his pale eyes grim. "Haven't you figured it out yet, Susan? The Blood Brothers are vampires."

Ten

Susan's laugh felt dry in her throat. It turned into a cough. "Of *course* they're vampires," she said. "That's why they call themselves Blood Brothers and wear those stupid dark glasses, pretending that the light hurts their eyes. It's all part of the act, like the name of their club. The Brothers are nothing but hype."

Drew shook his head, his eyes somber. "I'd give anything if that were so," he said, "but it's not. You're wrong, Susan. Dead wrong. I told you you'd have to believe. The Brothers are vampires. *Real* vampires."

Susan stared at him. "But that's not possible," she breathed. "I mean, vampires are superstition—folklore. Vampires are what they make movies out of, not rock bands."

Drew's voice was cynical. "Since when is it possible to be talking to a dead man on television?" he asked. "It doesn't make sense that Sara Robertson is dead, either—with a puncture wound on her throat."

A *puncture wound.* Susan's hands felt clammy, and she wiped them on her denim skirt. *The coroner never did explain the puncture wound.*

Drew's voice became gritty. "Bishop's errand here tonight was a vampire errand. How much sense does that make?"

"A vampire errand?" Susan repeated, her voice rising. She put her hand to her throat. "Are you saying he came for *me*? That's crazy!"

Drew's chuckle was bitter. "Of course it's crazy. That's why you have to throw out everything your mind is telling you about what can and cannot be. You have to *believe* in the irrational and in what you've always thought impossible."

"I can't," she said, beginning to cry. "I'm sorry, but I just can't."

"Then I can't help you," Drew said flatly. "Or Freddie, or Angela, or . . . wait, there's somebody else." He stopped, frowning. "I'm not getting her name. She's somebody's sister."

"Nita?"

"Yes, Juanita. I can't help her either."

Susan closed her eyes. The cold inside of her congealed into a hard, metallic-tasting fear, and she remembered the dread she'd felt at the club—the feeling that she'd said good-bye to Freddie and Angie and Brad and Nita for the last time.

Drew was speaking again, and Susan opened her eyes. "Your friend Brad is already gone," he said. "I don't think there's anything you can do about him. But the others—" He hesitated. "I can't say for sure, but if you act quickly, you might be able to save them. In order to help, though, you must not let yourself be taken."

Susan nodded solemnly. "Go on," she urged.

"The Brothers don't possess their victims all at once," Drew explained. "They take them little by little, over a period of several days. And their victims have to consent—that's one of the rules they operate under. As I said, they can't take what they aren't given."

With a shiver Susan thought of Freddie standing behind Flint earlier that night, her eyes fixed on him. Had she already consented? And if the Brothers could take all her friends, how would Susan be strong enough to resist?

Drew smiled crookedly. "Their methods can be pretty persuasive," he said, as if he were plugged into Susan's thoughts. "The music, for instance. Some people find it irresistible. The lyrics tell them anything they want to hear. The music promises them the freedom to do whatever they *feel* like doing."

Susan could feel herself trembling. Drew was right about the music. That was what had frightened her earlier at the club and then again when Bishop had come over. You could do anything you wanted and forget about paying the consequences.

Drew's mouth tightened. "If you move fast, Susan, if you get to your friends right away and tell them what you know about the Brothers, they might still be able to respond to you. Some of them, anyway."

Susan recoiled as if he'd hit her. "You mean, I'd have to tell them . . . what you told me?" How could she? How could she tell them that she'd gotten this urgent message about vampires from a dead man who appeared to her on television? "They'd think I've lost my mind," she whispered. "They'd never believe me."

"They might," Drew said quietly.

Susan shook her head. "This is idiotic. People in their right minds don't—"

Drew snorted. "There you go, being rational again. I tell you, the Brothers don't operate under the laws of reason." He paused. His tone got serious once again. "There's something else you have to do, Susan."

A half-hysterical giggle rose in Susan's throat. "I hope it's easier than believing."

"It's harder," Drew said grimly. "You have to keep yourself safe. If you're taken, your friends won't stand a chance."

"Taken?" The giggle came up again.

Drew's voice was hard-edged, grating. "You invited Bishop in, didn't you? That gives a vampire a carte blanche. It's one of the rules."

The giggle died. "Do you mean he can come in—anytime?"

"Whenever he wants."

Susan stared at him.

"This isn't a game, Susan." His face was stern, but sympathetic. "There are a lot of superstitions about vampires, as you know, and many of them are rooted in the truth. Garlic and roses and wild thyme, for instance. It's true. They'll ward off vampires. A cross works too, if you believe, and it's easier to find a cross than to happen on some wild thyme. If you don't already own a cross, get one. Put it on. And for heaven's sake, *never take it off*."

"I guess I could get one from Angie tomorrow. She has a lot of them."

"No, you can't wait that long. Bishop might be back tonight, and you need to be prepared. Make one out of a couple of matches. Better yet, make two or three. Put one by your bed. Hang one around your neck."

"But I—"

There was a loud, commanding knock at the door.

"Is it . . . him?" Susan asked.

"How should I know?" Drew asked. "I can't see through the door any more than you can."

Susan got up. "Excuse me," she said. She giggled again, at the idea of saying "excuse me" to a television set. Then she stopped giggling. She suddenly felt cold. If it was Bishop, she wouldn't let him in. She didn't have to tell him that she'd learned the truth about him. She could just say it was too late for company.

The knock came again. "Susan?" a harsh voice asked. "Susan? Open the door." It was Mack.

With a feeling of relief Susan went to the door and opened it. Mack was standing there in his uniform with his arms folded across his chest.

"What I want to know," he demanded abruptly, "is what you're doing entertaining company at this time of night."

"Mack," Susan said tiredly, "don't you have anything better to do than worry about me?"

"The car woke Betty up," Mack replied. "Spinning tires in the gravel, she said. Woke the kids up, too. She didn't want to come out here herself, but she told me about it when I got home just now." He scowled darkly. "It's one o'clock in the morning. And you're only seventeen, remember? I don't care if you have graduated from high

126

school—you're still my little sister, and I'm still responsible for you."

"I'm sorry, Mack." Susan knew he was only doing what he thought was right. "I didn't invite him to come over. He just showed up. And he stayed only a few minutes. I asked him to leave." It was *almost* the truth.

"Yeah, well . . . ," Mack growled. He managed to give the impression that he was taking her explanation under consideration and he might—just *might*—accept it.

Susan sat down hard on the sofa. "It's late, Mack. And my friend's gone. Can we all go to bed now?"

Mack harrumphed. "All right." He headed toward the door. Then he paused and turned to face Susan again. "Oh, one more thing," he said as if he just remembered something. "Pete Dupree asked Betty and me to go fishing tomorrow on his boat. Can you keep the kids?"

Susan smiled. So Mack had an ulterior motive for coming up here at one in the morning. "Sure," she said. "I'd be glad to baby-sit."

"So you know, there's a tropical storm coming up the Gulf from the Yucatan. If it hits around here, it'll churn up the bottom and ruin the fishing for a couple of weeks. This may be our last chance for a while, so we'll probably take advantage of the situation and might not be back until dark."

127

"Stay as late as you like. I don't have any plans."

"Thanks." Mack was gruff, but placated. "And listen," he added, as a parting shot, "tell your friends that you don't have company after midnight. If they want to know why, tell them your brother says so, and he's a cop." He looked at her. "You got that?"

"I got it," Susan said with a small smile. She wondered what he'd say if she told him that the guy who'd spun his tires was a vampire. Maybe he'd get out his gun and threaten to shoot. Susan wondered if it would do any good if he did. Could a vampire be killed by an ordinary bullet? She seemed to remember something about silver bullets—but where did you get a silver bullet?

She caught herself, feeling trapped in the absurdity of her questions. She was acting as if what Drew had told her was real. She was acting as if *Drew* was real. But still—

Mack was halfway down the stairs when she called to him. "Uh, Mack, what ever happened with Sara Robertson?"

Mack turned around. "Who?"

"The girl they found in the motel last week. The girl who followed the rock band down here from Dallas."

Mack frowned. "How'd you know about that?

I thought her family was keeping the whole thing a secret. They didn't want it getting out that their daughter turned into a groupie, so they've been keeping it out of the papers."

Drew Morris, the dead guy on the beach, told me, Susan wanted to say. But she only shrugged, making her voice sound casual. "I don't know. I must have heard it at work. News gets around." She swallowed. "What . . . was the name of the band?"

"Blood something. Yeah, Blood Brothers. That was it. Pete is handling the investigation, and he brought the bandleader in for questioning. He turned out clean. Anyway, the girl died of natural causes. There wasn't any crime."

Susan stood still, feeling the blood pound in her temples. "Oh," she said.

"Betty will send the kids out about nine," Mack said. "You got stuff for breakfast?"

"Yes," Susan replied absently. When Mack got to the foot of the stairs, she shut the door and put the chain on, moving slowly and deliberately. Then she turned around.

"Drew?" she asked.

The television screen was blank. Drew was gone.

Before she went to bed, Susan stood by the phone a few minutes, debating whether she should call Angie and Freddie. But the thought that the phone would wake up their parents kept her from doing it. Anyway, what would she ask them once she managed to get them on the line? *You haven't been bitten by a vampire lately, have you, Freddie?* Or *Remember, Angie—to keep a vampire away, just say no.* The thought made her smile, but the smile faded immediately.

Susan slept very little that night. She dreamed once of Drew. He was standing on the beach, holding his arms out to her. She ran toward him, laughing, happy to be with him, eager for his arms around her. But just as she reached him, he began to fade into transparency, only to reappear at the top of a dune, beckoning to her with an enigmatic smile. She started toward him, but the way was suddenly blocked by Flint and Brad and the other Brothers. Flint gestured toward a white sheet-covered mound at his feet. Fearfully, she lifted a corner of the sheet. Under it were the bodies of Freddie, Angela, and Nita, still and waxy-white, each with a puncture wound in her throat.

As she opened her mouth to scream, Drew was standing beside her, touching her. "To save them," he said, "you have to believe."

Susan's scream was a whimper. "I believe in you. *You* save them."

"I wish I could," Drew said sadly, "but I can't.

You're the only one who can save them. To do it, you have to trust yourself, believe in the Brothers, and control the power."

With that, he was gone.

Eleven

When Susan got up the next morning and looked at herself in the bathroom mirror, she saw dark circles under her eyes. She put on some extra cover-up. Even if nobody was going to be around but the kids, she didn't want to be reminded of how little she had slept.

"I'll have pancakes for breakfast," seven-year-old Pete announced.

"French toast," Randy asserted. He scowled at Pete. "I'm older. You have to eat what I say." Randy was nine.

"I say we're going to have fried-egg sandwiches," Susan said, getting out the skillet, "and I'm older than both of you put together." The boys couldn't quarrel with that logic and played quietly while Susan cooked. After breakfast she sent them out in the yard to play pirates with the toy swords and daggers they'd brought from El Paso, with the promise that later they would go to the video store and rent a movie.

Susan was glad for the day off from work, more so than on any other Sunday when the Pizzeria was closed. And since the kids pretty much took care of themselves, she had plenty of time to herself—to tidy up, do some laundry, and *think*.

Of course she'd heard stories about the supernatural, she thought, as she rinsed out her red blouse and hung it on the line across the back porch. She smiled at Randy, who waved to her from the swing set where he was hanging upside down by his knees, his dagger in his hand. She'd read about vampires and evil demons in *Dracula* and *Dr. Jekyll and Mr. Hyde*. She'd seen vampire movies, too. But all that stuff was fiction. Some interesting, some boring, but all of it the product of somebody's imagination.

But she couldn't see how Drew's appearance on the television set could be a product of her imagination. Freddie had seen him, and so had Bishop. Bishop had even recognized him, a fact that came as close to confirming Drew's story as anything else. And Mack had verified the rest of it—the part about Sara Robertson being a groupie of the Blood Brothers. And if that was true, wasn't it logical that the *whole thing* was true?

Wasn't it logical that the Blood Brothers were vampires?

Susan could admit the possibility of a reality beyond the one she knew, and she could admit—because she had *felt* it—that the Blood Brothers and their music were dangerous, but she still couldn't believe in vampires. It was too ridiculous.

After giving Randy and Pete a snack that they claimed was for the crocodiles in the moat, and sending them back outside, Susan picked up the phone and called Angie's house.

"Angie and Nita are still asleep," her mother said. "They got in very late last night, you know. So late, in fact, that neither of them could get up for Mass this morning." She sounded angry, and it seemed that she blamed Susan.

At Freddie's the phone rang and rang. She finally answered, sounding very groggy. Too groggy to talk, really. She'd had a late night, and she was planning to sleep all day. "I'll see you tomorrow," she said, yawning, and clumsily hung up the phone.

So much for being in danger, Susan told herself, putting down the phone. *So much for vampires.* She couldn't decide whether she felt foolish or just plain relieved.

The kitchen door opened. "Hey, Susan," Randy yelled as he and Pete burst into the room, "we

135

need some more peanut butter and crackers."

"More?" Susan asked, laughing. "Those crocodiles must be very hungry today."

"It's not for them," Pete said happily. He climbed on a chair to get the box of crackers. "It's for our new friend. He's a pirate, too."

Susan frowned. "What friend?"

"Me," a voice said.

Susan whirled, startled. "Who—? Oh, you."

Brad grinned lazily at her, the light glinting off his dark glasses. "Yeah, me," he said, leaning his shoulder against the doorjamb, looking relaxed in his black turtleneck and black jeans. "I was driving by and thought I'd stop and say hi. The boys invited me in."

"Invited you in?" Susan swallowed. *That gives a vampire carte blanche. It's one of the rules.*

"Yeah," Brad said. He tousled Randy's hair. "Randy and me, we're buddies, right?"

"He's Jean Lafitte the pirate," Randy shouted, brandishing his red plastic dagger. "And I'm his loyal mate. Come on, Pete, hurry up with the crackers. The ship's about to leave."

Pete turned to Susan and said, "Brad's going up in the tree house with us. We're going to have a picnic."

Susan frowned. Drew had said that Brad was already one of them, and in her dream he had been with the other Brothers, standing over the

136

bodies of her friends. But now that he was here, leaning against her door, all that seemed pretty silly. Brad was a real, live person, not a vampire. But somehow she still didn't trust him.

"Wait a minute, guys," Susan told the boys. "Your ship's not going anywhere—except to the video store."

"The video store?" Pete climbed down from the chair. "Super! Can we have popcorn too? Come on, Randy. Race you to the car!"

"Hey, I'm a video freak," Brad said. "What are you going to get?"

"*Captain Hook*," Randy shouted. "Want to watch it with us, Brad?" Before waiting for an answer, Randy dropped his dagger and dashed out of the room and down the back stairs after Pete.

"Uh, you can't," Susan said quickly. She gave the first excuse she could think of. "I mean, I can't ask you to stay. I'm not supposed to have company when I'm baby-sitting."

Brad grinned. "You're old enough to live by yourself, but you're not old enough to have company while you're baby-sitting? Come off it, Suzie."

Susan reached for her purse. "No," she said. "And my name is Susan. Now, if you'll excuse me, I need to lock up." She went through the living room to bolt the front door. Brad was still there when she came back into the kitchen, leaning against the door.

"Bishop said to tell you hi," he said carelessly.

Susan took a deep breath. "Tell him hi back for me," she said in the most casual tone she could manage. She frowned a little. It was hot outside today, and humid—good tropical-storm weather. Why was Brad wearing a turtleneck?

"I will," Brad said. "He was a little bummed by what happened last night, you know."

Susan went past Brad through the door and stood waiting for him to follow her out. "He was?" she asked. She wondered about just how much Brad knew about what had happened the night before. Would Bishop have told the others about Drew Morris?

"Yeah," Brad said. The corners of his mouth tightened. "So was Flint, when he heard about it. He asked me to give you a message, Suzie."

Susan reached past him to close the door, but he put his hand on her arm. "I said, I have a message from Flint," he repeated. There was a clear threat in his voice.

"What kind of message?" Susan asked quietly.

"He said to tell you to stay away from Angie and Freddie and Nita," he said. "He thinks you're a bad influence on them."

Susan's eyes widened in disbelief. "What? Who does he think he is, telling me to—"

"Hey, cool it, Suzie." Brad's voice was smooth, soft. "I'm trying to make this easy for you. I don't

138

want you to get hurt, so I'm telling you this for your own good, okay? Nobody's going to involve you in anything if you don't want to be involved. We're not going to force you to hang out with us, or even to come to the club. Everybody's got free will, you know? All you have to do is stay out of the picture and you're home free. It's that simple."

From the driveway Susan could hear her nephews honking the horn. "Hey, Susan! Let's go!" Randy yelled. "Pete and me are tired of waiting."

"I've got to go," Susan said, trying to free herself from Brad's grasp.

Brad's fingers tightened on Susan's arm. "You do know," he said softly, "that you can always get in the picture yourself." He released her arm, and stepped back. "There's always room for another fan. Sometimes people don't like our music at first and change their minds later, after they've really listened to it. You know what I mean?"

Susan looked at him. What was he saying? Was he really talking about the music or—

"I'm not sure," she said.

Brad nodded. "Well, hey, that's a start," he said encouragingly. "If you're not sure, maybe you ought to try listening to the music again sometime." He turned and went down the stairs ahead of her, and stopped at the car.

"Hey, guys," he said, "thanks for the invitation.

I can't stay for the movie, but maybe I'll be back to see you. What do you think? Do you want me to come?"

Susan stepped forward, but before she could say anything, the boys had chorused a loud "Yeah!" and Randy had added, generously, "You can come *anytime*, Brad."

Twelve

Susan had already finished putting out the stuff for the salad bar when Freddie finally made it into work on Monday. Angie, who was usually very punctual, hadn't shown up yet, and Susan was really starting to get worried.

"How are you?" Susan asked Freddie. It wasn't a casual question.

Freddie rubbed her eyes. "Sleepy," she said. Her cap was crooked, and she was putting on her apron wrong side out. "Tired. Worn out. Pooped. How are you?"

"You've got your apron on backward," Susan said gently. "Were you out late last night?"

"No." With an effort Freddie reversed her apron. "The club isn't open on Sunday night. We practiced for a couple of hours in the evening, and I got to bed early for a change." She gave Susan a wry smile. "Mom saw to that. She's put her foot down about the late hours. I guess I'm going to have to tell the guys that we've got to start practicing earlier." She took a pair of sunglasses out of her apron pocket and put them on.

"What's the matter with your eyes?" Susan asked, a small buzz of alarm sounding inside her.

Freddie shrugged. "Nothing serious," she said. "They just feel a little gritty, that's all. These glasses aren't really dark enough, but they're all I figure I can get by with on the job. Knowing Gwen, she'll probably have something to say about them." With a sigh she picked up a stack of plates and started out of the kitchen. "All I know is I could really use a day off. I've got an incredible headache."

Susan was slicing mushrooms when Angie arrived. She was walking slowly, shoulders slumped, feet dragging. Her face was pale and her eyes shadowed.

"I'm sorry I'm late," she said listlessly. "I slept right through the alarm." She looked around. "Has Gwen hit the roof yet?"

"She's not even here," Susan replied. She cleared her throat. "Uh, did you and Nita go over to the Brothers' house on Saturday night after the show?"

Angie brightened. "Yeah. You should have come too, Susan. They've got a great house. We had a terrific time."

"What did you do?" Susan asked. She began slicing peppers, watching Angie out of the corner of her eye.

Angie smiled vaguely. "Oh, danced, that's all. And listened to music." She sighed, eyes half-closed. "Brad gave me a tape of the Brothers' music. Nita and I have been listening to it all weekend."

Susan frowned. "But I thought you didn't like rock."

"I thought I didn't either. I like the Brothers' music, though," Angie said, picking up a knife. "It makes me feel . . ." Her voice trailed off.

"Makes you feel how?" Susan persisted.

Angie began to slice onions for the pizza topping. "I don't know." She shrugged. "Like it lets me be myself, maybe."

Susan pushed the peppers into a bowl. "I don't understand," she said.

Angie turned. "That's because you didn't really listen to the music the other night," she said angrily. "If you did, you'd know what I'm talking about. But you won't listen. You're afraid the music might *do* something to you." Her voice was almost a sneer. "You're afraid the music might make you drop that phony I'm-so-good, I'm-

143

totally-in-charge act and find out what you're really all about down deep inside. You'll find out you've got the freedom to do what you feel like doing, and that it's good for you." She eyed Susan. "Yeah, that really freaks you out, doesn't it?"

Susan stared at her friend. In all the time she'd known Angie, she'd never heard that ugly tone of voice. And what Angie was saying about the music was exactly what Drew had said.

Angie turned away again, as if she were struggling with herself. She dragged the back of her hand across her eyes. "I'm sorry, Susan," she muttered. "I didn't mean any of that—I don't even know where it came from. Forget it, will you?"

"That's okay," Susan replied. She frowned. "What's wrong with your eyes, Angie?"

"It's the onions," Angie said tonelessly. But her eyes stayed red-rimmed and bloodshot for the rest of their shift, and Susan never saw her smile.

Mack came in on his lunch hour for a pizza. "Hey, thanks for baby-sitting yesterday," he said. "The kids had a great time."

"I enjoyed it too," Susan said, ringing his sale on the register, "although I have to admit that I started getting a little seasick the third time through *Captain Hook*. How was your day? Did you guys catch anything yesterday?"

Mack handed her a ten. "Not much. Probably the storm. They named it today—Clarissa." He frowned. "Hey, listen, if it blows in along the coast here, I want you to close up that apartment and stay with us in the house. You hear?"

Susan laughed. "What makes you think," she asked teasingly, "that your house is any safer than the garage apartment?"

"Nice try," Mack said. His mouth was set stubbornly. "I don't care if it makes sense. I want you with us. If they order an evacuation to the mainland, I don't want to waste time looking for you."

"Okay," Susan said. She went to get Mack's iced tea. Her brother could be a pain, but it was good to know that he was looking out for her. It made her feel connected to something. Suddenly she wondered whether Freddie and Angie still felt that way about their families. She thought maybe they didn't. She handed Mack the glass.

"You got any lemon?"

Susan found it for him.

"And did you tell your friend about the no-company-after-midnight rule?"

"I haven't seen him," Susan replied. "But I'll tell him when I do."

Mack shifted his big bulk, looking uncomfortable. "Sorry for giving you such a hard time Saturday night," he said gruffly.

"It's okay," Susan said softly. If she could have reached him, she would have hugged him.

Later on that evening Nita came in. Susan was

surprised when she saw her. Nita's olive-toned skin looked sallow, and her face was drawn and tired looking. She was wearing a sleeveless top with a high collar.

"Angie," Susan said in the kitchen, "is Nita okay?"

"What do you mean 'okay'?" Angie asked defensively. She grabbed a plate off the stack. It slipped through her fingers, and she muttered something under her breath as she bent to pick up the pieces.

Susan was startled. She had never heard Angie curse before. She reached for the broom. "I mean," she said carefully, "is Nita feeling all right? She looks like she's got the flu or something."

"Yeah, she's got the flu," Angie said, ignoring the broom. "So butt out, okay?" She flung the pieces of the broken plate into the trash.

Susan leaned the broom against the wall and put both hands on Angie's shoulders. "I'm not going to butt out," she said quietly. "Something's going on with you guys, and I want to know what it is. I want to help you." She touched Angie's face. "I'm not telling you what to do or anything. I just care, that's all."

Angie's face softened. "I'm sorry," she whispered. "I don't know what's gotten into me today. I guess maybe I'm coming down with Nita's flu, too." Then something seemed to happen inside her, and the tenderness went out of her face and voice. She stepped back. "I said, *butt out*, Susan," she said flatly. "We don't need your help."

Susan was exhausted when she got home. Tourist season had started with a bang, and the Pizzeria had been packed all day. Freddie had left at four because of her headache, and even though Angie had stuck it out for the entire shift, she hadn't done anything right. Covering for Freddie and Angie, Susan had done three times the work she normally did, and when she climbed the stairs to her apartment, she was so tired she could hardly move.

Once inside, Susan went into the living room and sat down heavily. She was trying not to think of Freddie's pained face and the flat, ugly sound of Angie's voice when she'd told her to butt out. She was trying not to think of Drew, either, or of the things he had said. She had always prided herself on being reasonable and logical. How could she believe him?

But she couldn't stop thinking. She kept remembering Angie's accusation that she hadn't really listened to the music, that she'd been afraid of what the lyrics might tell her. It was true. She *was* afraid of the Brothers' music. She'd been afraid of it at the club on Saturday night, and later, when Bishop came over and put a tape on the player.

But there was something in it that made Angie and Freddie act the way they were acting, and she had to find out what it was. Listening to the music, Susan decided, really concentrating on the words, was the only way to find out.

Susan smiled a little, thinking of Mack and his worries. If he knew about this, he'd tell her not to listen—he hated rock, anyway. If Drew were here, he'd certainly tell her not to listen. But she wasn't responsible to them, she was responsible to herself. And her heart told her that if the music was exerting some strange influence over her friends, she had to find out what it was.

What are you up to tonight, Susan?

Oh, nothing much. Listening to a little vampire music, that's all.

Still, it was something she had to do. Moving very deliberately, she went into the other room and turned all the lights off except the desk lamp. She stood for a moment looking down at the television set. She unplugged it and walked over to the tape player. Standing there, she remembered how frightened she had felt when Bishop played the tape before. She remembered that she'd wanted to put her fingers in her ears and shut the music out. This time she had a reason to listen to it. She switched on the player and turned the volume up high. Then she forced herself to pull up the chair in front of the speaker. She sat down in it, closed her eyes, and began to listen. For the first time she really *heard* the words.

Yes, they promised freedom, freedom from everything she'd ever thought or learned. They promised that you could do what you wanted to do, that you didn't have to follow anybody's rules but your own. They made sense. They made perfect sense. And they made you feel powerful, so powerful that you knew you could conquer the world. All you had to do was—

The tape had stopped playing when Susan realized, dimly, that someone was knocking at the door. With difficulty she roused herself, forcing her eyes open. It was late, after eleven, and she didn't feel like answering the door, no matter who it was. Anyway, why should she? It was her house, and she could do things *her* way. Right now all she wanted to do was listen to the music. She got up to turn the tape over.

But the knock came again, louder and more commanding. Maybe she'd better. The room seemed foggy, and she stumbled as she went toward the door. Sleepiness, that's what it was. Pushing pizzas all day had worn her out. She'd listen to the tape once more and then go to bed.

Susan saw that the chain was on. She smiled a little, holding on to the doorknob. That was good. It was good that she'd remembered to put on the chain. She was safe when the chain was on. She leaned her forehead against the door.

"Who is it?" she asked groggily.

The voice was soft. "Don't you know?"

Susan closed her eyes. "I . . . don't want to see you right now, Bishop." Her tongue felt thick. It was hard to speak.

"I know," Bishop said sympathetically. "It's been a long day, hasn't it? We don't have to talk, Susan. We can just sit quietly if you like." He paused. "We can do anything, you know. We can listen to some more music, if that's what you want."

Listen to music, Susan thought blurrily. Yes, that was a good idea, a very good idea. Listening to music would make her feel good. She fumbled the chain off and opened the door.

"Come in," she invited him.

"Thank you," Bishop said. He took off his dark glasses and smiled at her.

Thirteen

Bishop closed the door behind him and put the chain on. He turned around to face Susan.

"Not expecting big brother tonight?" he remarked casually.

Susan licked her lips. They were very dry. "I don't . . . maybe," she said.

Bishop glanced at the television, saw that it was unplugged. "Ah," he said. He nodded knowingly. His smile grew.

Suddenly Susan was afraid, and the fear cleared away some of the fog. She caught her lower lip between her teeth, feeling cold, feeling her hands grow clammy.

"Go away," she said. "It's getting late. I have to—"

"But you played the music," Bishop said softly. He took a step toward her. His eyes were dark and deep, his voice rich and compelling. "You invited me. You must want me here, or you wouldn't have invited me in."

Don't invite any of them into your house. It was Drew's warning. She should have remembered! She should have made the crosses he told her to make, too. Susan stepped back, away from the hypnotic darkness in Bishop's eyes. But she couldn't back up any farther. She was against the wall, beside the open window.

"I want you to go away," she repeated. She raised her voice, hearing it thin and reedy, close to hysteria. "I take back my invitation. Go away!"

"Let me kiss you," Bishop said gently, taking another step toward her. "You'll see, Susan—it's not so bad. You'll like it. Your friends do. They want you to be with them, Susan. They want us all to be together. He wants it too. He commands it."

"He?" Susan whispered, the fear washing over her in a numbingly icy wave.

"The One who commands us." Bishop's eyes gleamed. He smiled. "A kiss, Susan. One kiss." He took another step toward her.

Susan stood still, captured by Bishop's eyes. She felt herself waver, wanting to take a step forward, wanting to feel his arms around her. Perhaps, if he held her, she wouldn't feel so afraid.

She could join Freddie and Angie. And then, with a shudder, she remembered the sheet-covered mound in her dream, the waxy-white bodies under, and Drew standing beside her.

"*Don't move.*" The command was firm, sharp. The voice came out of the empty air beside her. Susan wrenched her eyes away from Bishop's to her right. The figure beside her was dim and shadowy, nearly transparent. Drew!

A grimace twisted Bishop's face. His eyes blazed. "What are you doing here?" he hissed.

Drew raised his voice. "In the name of everything that's good and loving, I command you to leave."

Bishop laughed, a mocking cackle that raised goose bumps on Susan's arms. "You're too late with your mumbo jumbo, Morris. The lady's already asked me in, not just once, but twice. You know the rules." He stepped forward and raised his arms protectively over Susan. "She's mine, and you can't do anything about it. You're only a ghost, Morris. I can see right through you." His lips stretched across white teeth in a triumphant smile, his voice became richly gloating. "I am the Undead, and this one is mine!"

Susan's eyes widened. On the floor under the lamp table she could see one of her nephews' toys—the red plastic dagger Randy had been playing with while he watched *Captain Hook*. The blade and the handle came together in the form of a cross.

Without thinking what she was doing, she swept the dagger from the floor. Seizing it by the blade, she held it out in front of her.

"Go!" she cried. She lunged forward and thrust the plastic dagger into Bishop's face.

There was a flash of blue fire, and then Bishop's agonized scream filled the room with a horrible sound. He fell backward against a chair, knocking it to the floor with a crash. His flesh was seared where the cross had touched his cheek. Then he launched himself forward in a writhing, twisting dive through the window. In the darkness outside Susan could see a sudden flash; then there was nothing but a dying scream.

Susan shut her eyes. When she opened them, she saw the cross in her hands pulsing with a powerful blue light. Then it died away, and she was holding a red plastic dagger.

"Hey," the voice beside her said, "not bad for a beginner."

Susan turned. She could see the outline of Drew's figure in the dimness. It had bulk, solidity. It looked almost real.

"I . . . I—" She stopped, swallowed, tried again. "Did that really happen? Is he gone?"

"Yes, it happened. And yes, he's gone." He smiled. "You've killed one of the Undead, Susan.

You probably won't get a medal of honor, but it's quite an achievement anyway."

"Thanks," Susan managed. She swallowed again, her mouth dry as dust. She looked at him. The outlines of his body were firm, sharp, clear. She couldn't see through him anymore. "Are you really . . . ?" She couldn't finish her question.

"Really a ghost?" Drew looked down at his hand, flexed his fingers. "Well, I thought so. But now I'm not so sure." Wonderingly, he raised his hand and touched her face, very gently. "I can feel your skin, Susan. Can you feel my fingers?"

Susan shut her eyes. "Yes," she whispered. "I can feel your fingers." Her skin tingled where Drew was touching it. "Does that mean you're not a . . ."

"Don't ask me," Drew said. "I'm not writing the script for this show."

Susan opened her eyes again. Drew was leaning toward her, his eyes on her mouth, as if he were going to kiss her. Then he straightened up.

"I think," he said softly, "I'd better not press my luck."

Susan shivered. "How did you get here?"

"Beats me." Drew sounded wryly amused. "Didn't you invite *me*, too?"

Susan remembered her thought of the sheet-covered mound she had dreamed, with Drew standing beside her. "Did you materialize when I thought about you? Just like that?"

Drew looked down at her, smiling. "That's what it looks like," he said. "But I don't know how. I'm not in charge here." His voice was getting fainter, the outline of his figure blurry.

"Drew," Susan whispered urgently, "don't go away! I need you. I need to know what to do next! I've got to help Freddie and Angie."

"I said, I'm not in charge here," Drew's voice said, sounding faint and tinny. She could almost see through him again, see the outline of the sofa and the chair behind him. "I'll get back to you."

"But when?"

"When I can. From now on I guess it depends on you."

"Wait a minute, Drew," Susan said desperately, reaching out for him. "*What* depends on me?"

"Whether I get back to you," he said in a soft voice. "You have the power. You have to learn how to use it." He seemed to make an effort, and the outlines of his image grew sharper. "Talk to Angie's aunt," he added more clearly. "She can help."

And then he was gone.

The next morning Susan was awakened at nine by the shrill ringing of her telephone.

"Did you watch the weather report last night?" Mack asked, not even saying hello.

"No," Susan replied groggily. After Drew had disappeared, she had made a rude cross out of two ice-cream sticks. Then she'd gone to bed, with Randy's plastic dagger under her pillow. Sleep was slow in coming, though, because her mind was searching for ways to help Freddie and Angie break free of the Brothers. But all her searching ended in murky blackness. She couldn't see any way out.

Mack's voice was brisk, businesslike. "Hurricane Clarissa is heading inland. They're forecasting landfall on the Texas coast, somewhere between Freeport and Port Arthur. That puts us in the middle. It'll be here by three o'clock this afternoon."

Susan sat up.

"They're calling it a Class Three," Mack said, "so we don't have to evacuate here in the city. But the entire police force is being called in, so I've got to work. I want you in the house with Betty and the kids, so I know where you are. Call the Pizzeria and tell them you won't be in. They may not even open today, anyway."

Susan shook her head to clear it. "I've got some things to do before the storm hits," she said.

"Fine. Do them and get back here by one. Okay?"

"Okay," Susan said slowly. She got up and pulled on jeans and a T-shirt. She was thinking of Drew, and the way he'd looked last night when

157

he'd seemed about to kiss her. How did it feel to be kissed by a ghost? When he'd touched her, his fingers had seemed so *real*, and there'd been a wondering look in his eyes, as if he could actually feel the softness and warmth of her skin.

She shook her head, pushing the memory away. She couldn't think of Drew now. She had work to do. As she fastened her long brown hair into a ponytail, a vague plan began to form in her mind. She called work and told Gwen she wouldn't be in. As she got ready to leave, she stuck Randy's red plastic dagger into the belt on her jeans, under her T-shirt.

Outside, the air was still and heavy with the weight of the oncoming storm. The sky overhead was metallic, filled with gray clouds, and the sun wore a silvery halo. As Susan drove past the supermarket on the corner, she saw people scurrying around in prehurricane excitement, buying emergency supplies—extra food, candles, water. But Susan had a different emergency on her mind. She couldn't even think about the hurricane.

It was after ten by the time she got to Angie's house. Mrs. Sanchez was outside, fastening the hurricane shutters over the windows. At the house next door Aunt Carlota was doing the same thing. The two women were talking over the hedge about the storm.

When Aunt Carlota saw Susan, she waved.

"Good morning," she said, climbing down from the ladder. "Ready for the big storm?"

"If you're here to see Angela," Mrs. Sanchez said, "she's still in bed." She scowled. "She called in sick to work this morning."

Aunt Carlota came over to the hedge. "I saw her yesterday afternoon at the Pizzeria. She looked awfully tired."

"Is she all right?" Susan asked.

Mrs. Sanchez fastened the last shutter. "She's just worn out. She and Juanita were over at that club again last night. When they got home, their father told them they can't go back. I don't think it's good for girls to be out so late, either."

"We were young once, too," Aunt Carlota said knowingly. "I'm sure it's nothing to worry about."

Mrs. Sanchez shook her head apprehensively. "I tell you, 'Lota, I don't understand it. Angela's always been so good. I could always count on her to do what's right. But the last three days—it's like she's a different person. Juanita, too."

"Would it be all right if I went in to see her?" Susan asked Mrs. Sanchez.

"Go right ahead. Maybe *you'll* be able to figure out what's wrong."

Susan went into the house and down the hall to Angela's room. She could hear the Brothers' music through the door. She opened it. "It's me, Angie," she said. "Susan."

"I don't want to see you," Angie replied. "Get out of here. Go away."

With a quick step Susan went to the tape player and jabbed the off button savagely. Then she reached for the cord and snapped up the blind. What she saw on the bed made her gasp.

Angie was haggard, her face white, her eyes red-rimmed and circled with dark flesh. When the light struck her eyes, she shielded them with her hand.

"Pull the blind down!" she said hoarsely, groping for a pair of dark glasses on her bedside table. "And turn the tape back on!"

Susan dropped the blind down and sat on the side of Angie's bed. "Do you know what's happening to you?" she asked quietly.

Angie leaned back against her pillow. "Happening?" she asked, putting on her sunglasses. "Nothing's happening. I'm finding out who I really am for the first time in my life, that's all. Brad and the Brothers . . ." She smiled slyly. "Really, Susan, you're totally missing out. I don't see why you won't—"

Susan grabbed her by the shoulders. "Don't you know what they are?" she cried desperately. "Don't you know what they're doing to you?" She shook Angie's shoulders, hard. Her head flopped back loosely, like the head of a rag doll. There were two faint red marks—*puncture marks*—on her throat.

Susan dropped her hands, feeling sick.

"But I *like* it," Angie whispered. Her mouth was trembling. A muscle in her cheek twitched. "I like listening to the music. I like going to the club. I want to be with Brad and the Brothers always." She smiled a strange, slow smile. "Brad says it'll be only another night or two before I'm one of them. Then I'll feel better, he says. I won't be so sick and draggy all the time. This is a phase I'm going through. After tonight I'm sure I'll feel better."

Susan caught her breath. "But what about your parents? Your mother said your father's forbidden you to go back to the club."

Angie's laugh was shrill. "You think I'm going to let that old man order me around?" She stopped laughing, and her face took on a crafty, cunning look. "I'm leaving, anyway. I'm going to move in with Brad tomorrow. That way I'll be able to spend all my time with the Brothers. I'll be able to listen to their music whenever I feel like it." Her mouth twisted. "Without people barging in and turning it off."

Susan took her hands and held them. "What about Nita?"

Behind the dark glasses Angie's eyes slid sideways. "What about her?" she mumbled. "Nita's okay."

"Where is she?"

"At the Brothers' house. She came in here this

morning and climbed out my window so Mom wouldn't see her leave."

"Does she look like you?" Susan asked bluntly.

Angie frowned. "What?"

Susan snatched off Angie's glasses. She dragged her out of bed and propelled her toward the dressing table beside the window, where she pushed her down on the bench in front of the mirror and jerked up the blind. Angie's bloodshot eyes stared into the mirror, her hair hanging in matted strings around her pale face. The muscle in her cheek twitched violently.

"Is this what you want for your sister?" Susan whispered.

Angie stared defiantly at her reflection. "What's wrong with the way I look?" she asked. "I'm a little tired, that's all. It's part of the process. Brad says I'll feel better soon. The same thing happened to him, when he became one of the Brothers." She grinned, showing white teeth. "After tonight I'll feel wonderful. Brad promised."

Susan shuddered. "You can't let this happen, Angie!" she cried. "If you don't care about yourself, you have to care about Nita!"

Angie swiveled to face Susan, her eyes narrowed, the pupils tiny slits of black. "If that's all you came for, Susan, to tell me what I can and can't do, you might as well leave. If I didn't listen to my father, what makes you think I'll listen to

162

you? I'm not going to give up Brad and the Brothers. Not for Nita, and certainly not for you."

Susan felt a deep, exhausting despair. She couldn't reach Angie. It was too late. And if it was too late for Angie, it was probably too late for Freddie and Nita, too.

And then she remembered Randy's plastic dagger. She pulled it out of the belt and held it up like a cross. The plastic began to glow an eerie blue, as if it were lit from the inside. Susan could feel a throbbing current of energy pulsing from the cross through her arms and across her back. She pulled herself up, feeling tall and strong. Was this what Drew had meant when he said *You have the power*?

Angela's eyes widened and she shrank back, her arm up to shield her face. "Don't," she whispered. "Please, don't!"

When she spoke, Susan's voice was not her own. It came from a force outside her, speaking through her, strong and commanding.

"In the name of everything that's good and loving," she said, "I command you to depart from evil!"

Angie's muscles tensed, her face twisted in pain. Her body convulsed with a terrible, racking shudder. Susan wanted to turn away, but her curiosity kept her eyes riveted on her friend. Finally Angie collapsed onto the dressing table, limp, breathing in shallow gasps. Susan dropped the

163

dagger and held Angie's hand as tightly as she could. As she waited, a tiny spot of color came into Angie's cheeks. Susan could also see that the puncture marks in her friend's throat were beginning to fade.

Susan stood looking down at Angie. She felt a strange, heady exhilaration, as if she were still charged with the energy that had flowed through her. She gripped Angie's hand harder. "Angie?" she whispered. "Are you all right?"

Angie slowly sat up, her eyes unfocused. "I . . . I think so," she managed. "What did you do?"

"I'm not sure," Susan said. She picked up the plastic dagger from the floor, and then she stuck it back into her belt. "I guess this toy has something pretty powerful in it."

Angie stared at the dagger. "It's not a toy," she whispered. "It's a . . . cross." A sudden understanding came into her eyes. "Is . . . *that* what I became? One of . . . them?"

Susan looked at her. "Almost," she said quietly. Angie needed to hear the truth. The ugly, hideous truth. "You almost became a vampire. But you're safe now." *At least I hope so,* she thought. A new, cold thought sliced through her. But was Angie safe? Was she back to her normal state for good? Or would she return to the condition she was in when Susan found her?

Angie dropped her face into her hands. "Oh,

164

Susan," she whispered, anguished, "what have I done? Not just to myself, but to Nita! Have you seen her? Is she okay? How could I—"

Susan knelt down and put her arms around Angie. "It wasn't your fault," she whispered. "It was the Brothers. They are evil. They want to corrupt everyone who hears their music. They want everyone to be like them."

Angie began to cry, long, shuddering sobs that shook her shoulders. Susan held her close and let her cry. Finally she sat up and reached for a tissue and blew her nose. "I must have been out of my mind," she said. "I thought I loved Brad, but it wasn't love—it was an obsession. I couldn't see what was happening to me, or to him, or . . ." Her voice trailed off.

"Do you think," Susan asked softly, "that Brad can come back?"

Angie's mouth trembled, and her eyes filled with tears again. "I . . . I don't think so," she whispered. "He wouldn't want to come back, now that he's tasted that incredible power. I think he's . . . gone."

"I'm sorry, Angie," Susan said.

Angie's chin firmed and she straightened her shoulders. "But if you got me back, can't we get Nita back too?" she said. "And Freddie." She stopped, looking suddenly afraid. "But how, Susan? You have no idea how powerful they are! How can we do it?"

Suddenly Susan saw a movement outside the window. She turned and looked across the narrow yard between the houses. Aunt Carlota was standing on the ladder, a frozen statue. She must have seen everything.

Susan pulled Angie up. "Get dressed," she ordered. *Talk to Angie's aunt*, Drew had said. *She can help.*

"Where are we going?" Angie asked, climbing into her jeans.

"We're going next door," Susan said, "to talk to a white witch."

Fourteen

"*Es milagro*," Aunt Carlota said quietly, beckoning them into the kitchen. "It is a miracle." She kissed each girl once on each cheek and then on the forehead.

"You saw," Susan said.

"Yes," Aunt Carlota replied, "I saw." She poured them each a cup of hot herb tea. "Now you can tell me the whole story."

It took only a few minutes for Susan to tell her everything, beginning with Drew's first appearance on the television and ending with the scene in Angie's bedroom.

When Susan finished, Aunt Carlota took a deep breath. "I have heard of demonstrations of such power as the one you practiced this morning," she said, "but never have I seen one. It is truly a miracle."

Susan wrapped both hands around her cup, warming her cold fingers. "It wasn't much," she said, embarrassed by the awe and admiration in Aunt Carlota's voice.

"Yes, it was." Aunt Carlota gave Susan a respectful look. "You are a powerful *curandera*, my child. A strong healer."

Susan shook her head firmly. "No," she said. "I'm no *curandera*." She pulled the toy dagger out of her belt and laid it on the table. "It was this. This was what killed Bishop. And saved Angie."

Aunt Carlota smiled. "The power," she said firmly, "is not in the instrument of healing but in the heart of the one who heals." She pointed to the jars of herbs that lined her kitchen shelves. "The potions and charms and amulets that *curanderas* use are important. But these objects are vested with the power of the healer, not the other way around." She touched Susan's dagger. "This little piece of plastic has only the power *you* give it, Susan. You must have faith—not in this, but in yourself. And in your incredible power."

You have the power. It was Drew's voice Susan heard, as clearly as if he stood at her shoulder. At the recollection she felt a sudden sense of longing. It was his belief in her, his reassurance, that made her strong. If he were here, she could face anything, no matter how frightening. She could even face Flint and the Brothers. But Drew wasn't here. And without him she felt very small, very much afraid, and very vulnerable.

"But even if I do have the power," she said in a low voice, "I don't know how to use it. All I did with Angie was say a few words. It was nothing."

"Yes, a few words. A few simple words. But they were words from the heart. They were words of love. The strength of good over evil is powerful when one believes. And when one has love."

Susan nodded solemnly. Drew had given her the gift of belief by making her face the truth. And love? Had he given her that, as well? She looked at Aunt Carlota. "But I don't know what to do. I don't know how to save Nita and Freddie. You have to help us."

"I will help," Aunt Carlota agreed, and Susan felt a tremendous sense of relief. She and Angie wouldn't have to go to the Brothers' house alone. Aunt Carlota would be there with them, with her magic.

Aunt Carlota went into the other room. When she came back, she held three silver crosses in one hand and a large quartz crystal and a cloth bag in the other. She hung one cross around Angie's neck and gave the other two to Susan.

"These are for Nita and Freddie," she said. "They can wear these for protection. You do not need one, since your dagger should serve you quite well." Next she handed the crystal and the cloth pouch to Susan. "These are for you."

"Will we . . . will we have to destroy the vampires?" Susan asked faintly, not even looking at what she'd been given. "Will we have to use . . . stakes?" She swallowed, remembering a gory scene from a movie. "Through the heart?"

"Their evil must be destroyed," Aunt Carlota said. She smiled slightly. "Legends about stakes through the heart are a way of explaining something to people who need a picture in order to be able to see. The vampires must be destroyed, but you do not need to use stakes." She nodded at the small pouch in Susan's hand. "In that bag I've given you wild thyme and rose petals to sprinkle in the doorway of the house. That will help to purify it. But there are no magic words and no magic agents I can give you, Susan. It is only *your* power that can purify. And the words must come from you. The crystal is an amulet. It will help keep *you* pure in the presence of great evil."

"Hey, wait," Susan said, suddenly apprehensive. "You're coming with us, aren't you?"

Aunt Carlota shook her head. "This is *your* task," she said emphatically. "It has been given to you to do, not to me. I can give you advice, but I cannot do the work. If I interfere, I might upset the balance and work against you."

"But I don't know what to *do*!" Susan protested. "I need you to teach me!"

"You do not need a teacher," Aunt Carlota said gently. "No one taught you how to bring back Angela—you trusted your heart. That is what you must do now, Susan. That is your power." Her face relaxed into a smile, and she touched Angie's arm. "Angela will be there. And your friend Drew. They will be your helpers." She cocked her head, listening to the wind. "Now, go quickly. The storm is coming."

Susan's insides knotted. She could see the faces of the Brothers in front of her, their eyes filled with an unimaginable power. What if she failed? What if the evil that was in the Brothers swallowed *all* of them? Her hands felt cold and clammy. "Maybe we should . . . wait," she whispered, "until after the storm is over."

Angie moved closer to Susan. Her face was taut, her eyes dark. The silver cross gleamed against her throat. "We can't wait," she said, reaching for Susan's hand. "After the storm it may be too late. Nita and Freddie need you *now*, Susan."

Aunt Carlota nodded. "It is your time to do battle," she said. "And the storm will concentrate your power."

"Concentrate it?" Susan asked uncertainly. "What do you mean?"

"I can't explain it. It is something you will have to experience for yourself. But be careful, my dear. There is danger to you, too. A *curandera* is a conduit for tremendous energy. You must be strong enough to channel that destructive power without letting it destroy you." She looked at Susan, her eyes direct, compassionate. "Hate destroys, Susan. To purify, you must love. Love is the undoing of evil."

"But I don't understand," Susan began.

"You will," Aunt Carlotta said simply.

Angie stood up. "Come on, Susan," she said urgently. "Let's go."

Susan stood too. "I guess I'm ready." *Ready or not, here I come, vampires. Armed with my trusty toy dagger.* She almost laughed aloud at the utter absurdity of it.

Aunt Carlota reached into a small clay bowl on the table. "There's one last thing," she said. She pulled something out of the bowl. "Put these in your pockets."

She had given each of them a handful of garlic cloves.

As Susan and Angie drove along Sea Wall Boulevard in the direction of Freddie's mother's motel, Susan sensed a gray restlessness in the sea. Breakers were beginning to surge onto the almost-deserted beaches. The waves were slow, lethargic, but they contained enormous power. The threat of a hurricane had sent the tourists scurrying home. The only people in the water now were the surfers, taking advantage of the rolling breakers to get in a few hours of extra-good surfing. Everybody else was busy stowing anything that might blow away and nailing big sheets of plywood over glass windows to protect them against breakage. There was no panic. People who lived in Galveston were used to taking precautions against the tropical storms that blew in from the Gulf.

"There won't be a can of soup left in this whole town in another hour," Angie said as they drove by a grocery jammed with shoppers.

"You're probably right," Susan replied bleakly, remembering Freddie's cheerful advice to stock up with plenty of soup in case of a hurricane. *Freddie*. What would they find when they got to Freddie's? After all, she and Brad had been with the Brothers the same amount of time. Worse, Freddie was in love with Flint. Would they be able to bring her back? Or was she gone, too?

Angie put her hand in her pocket and pulled out the garlic. "I wonder how this works. Is it supposed to hurt them? Stop them? Make them disappear?"

"I wonder," Susan said grimly, "*if* it works." She thought somberly about their small arsenal of weapons. A toy dagger, a crystal, a bag of herbs, a silver cross, and a few cloves of garlic. Superstitious nonsense, she would have said two weeks ago, even a week ago. But that was before. Before Bishop had catapulted out of a second-story window and vanished in a burst of fire. Before she had met Drew. Before she had seen Angie come back.

The parking lot in front of the Holiday Plaza Motel was almost empty. Freddie's mother was directing two men who were boarding up windows. Sudden gusts of wind whipped up from the beach, blew in their faces, and tossed the palms in front of the motel.

"Freddie?" Mrs. Gardner asked. "She's got the flu or something. I told her to go back to bed." She raised her voice. "Hey, Charlie, when you've finished that window, take the diving board off and stow it, will you?" She turned back to the girls. "Last big storm, the wind ripped the diving board off and sent it through the office window."

"We need to see Freddie," Susan said. "We won't stay long."

"Go ahead." Mrs. Gardner shrugged. "If you catch what she's got, don't say I didn't warn you." She frowned. "Tell Freddie I'm going to the grocery store. If I don't get there pretty quick, there won't be anything left."

"We'll tell her," Angie said.

The girls went up to the second floor, where Freddie and her mother had a two-bedroom suite overlooking the swimming pool. They stood outside Freddie's door for a moment, listening. Inside, they could hear the sound of the Brothers' music, then Freddie's voice, singing the lyrics.

Angie's face went white, and she covered her ears with her hands. "You've got to shut off that music," she whispered. "I don't think I can stand to listen to it."

"Stay out here until it's off," Susan instructed. She raised her hand and knocked at the door.

The music stopped. There was a silence. Susan knocked again, louder this time.

A chair scraped. "Go away, Mom," Freddie's voice said. She sounded irritated. "I told you, I don't want anything to eat. I'm practicing."

"It's me and Angie," Susan said. "We have to talk to you."

Another silence. "So talk," Freddie said finally. "What do you want?"

"Not through the door," Susan said. "We need to see you, Freddie."

"Buzz off," Freddie said. The music came on again, louder this time.

Angie's face twisted with pain, and she put her fingers in her ears. Susan pushed the door open and stepped into the room, closing the door behind her.

Inside, it was almost totally dark, except for the glow of a flickering candle. Freddie was sitting on her bed wearing black jeans and a black T-shirt. On the table beside her was the candle and her tape player. Susan stepped to the bedside table and with a quick motion grabbed the cassette from the recorder and began to rip out the tape. In seconds there was a loose mound of plastic spaghetti at her feet.

"It's okay, Angie," she called. "You can come in now." The door opened.

Freddie was staring at her. "You ruined my tape!" she wailed. "How am I supposed to practice if I don't have a tape?"

Angie flicked on the light switch, and the room was flooded with a bright light. With an anguished cry Freddie rolled over and buried her face in the pillow.

"Let us look at you," Susan said quietly, putting a hand on the pillow.

"I've had the flu," Freddie said. Her voice was muffled by the pillow. "The light hurts my eyes. Turn it off." A cough rattled dryly in her throat. "*Turn it off!*" she screeched.

Susan pulled the pillow down. "Oh, no," Angie whispered.

Freddie's eyes were deep, shadowy pools in her hollowed face. Her freckles stood out in sandy splatters against her pale skin. She had put on lipstick, but it was smeared garishly red across her strong white teeth.

Her hands shaking, Freddie pulled the neck of her T-shirt up to her chin. "I've been sick for a couple of days," she muttered, her voice cracking. "What did you expect—Madonna?"

Susan yanked Freddie's hands down. There was a red mark on her throat.

Angie sank down beside the bed and took Freddie's hands in hers. "Hurry, Susan," she urged. "*Hurry!* Do it now!"

"Do what?" Freddie asked, struggling to get away. "What are you trying to do? Let go of me, Angie!" She struggled harder, swinging her legs over the side of the bed, and managed to pull free. "Angie, you were with us. You wanted to be one of us. What's happened to you?" She caught sight of the cross around Angie's neck, and her eyes narrowed to dark slits. "I might have known," she spat. "Traitor!"

Angie stood up and put her arms around Freddie. "Please, Freddie," she begged, "let us—"

Suddenly Freddie lunged forward, shoving Angie to the floor. "You're not going to try any fancy tricks with me," she snarled. She stood in the middle of the floor, arms raised, fists clenched. "I am one with the Brothers!" she cried in a strong, resonant voice. "I call on you! Come, Brothers! Come to me now!"

There was a moment of silence. Outside, a fierce gust of wind rattled the motel sign as if it had been hit by a giant's fist. Inside, the temperature in the room plummeted. The air was filled with an electrical tension that almost crackled.

Susan's mouth was dry. "Are we too late, Angie?" she whispered fearfully. If Freddie was already one of them, the power might destroy her completely, as it had Bishop. Or perhaps Freddie could summon a stronger power—a power that could destroy them!

"I don't know," Angie said, picking herself up off the floor. Her eyes were wide in her white face. "But we have to try. Do it now, Susan!"

Suddenly there was another gust of wind, and the lights went off. It was dark in the room, except for the candle burning beside the bed. In its flickering light Freddie's shadow on the wall, arms upraised, head back, was the shadow of a monster.

Susan had no choice. She pulled out the dagger and stepped toward Freddie. The dagger began to flash with a brilliant blue light. As Susan held it up, it become a kind of lightning rod, drawing life from the enormous energy of the storm, growing brighter and brighter until it was blazing. Susan could feel the fierce power coursing through her, charging her. The hairs on her arms and neck were raised, and her skin tingled. Before her, Freddie raised her hands in front of her face to shield her eyes from the brilliant blue light.

"In the name of love," Susan cried in a firm,

clear voice, "I command the evil in you to be gone."

Freddie shrieked, a high, whistling scream, furiously defiant. "No!" she cried. "No, no, *no*! I am one with the Brothers!"

One with the Brothers? How could Freddie say that? How could she *want* to be one with the evil force that had destroyed Drew and Sara Robertson and Brad—and countless others? A powerful anger ignited inside Susan, racing through her, hot and remorseless, a force far stronger than anything she had ever felt in her life. Susan felt herself grow taller, stronger, invincible. With such anger, such hatred, she could destroy the Brothers and the evil they stood for! She could purify the world, cleanse it forever from the horrible darkness of—

Hate destroys, Susan. To purify, you must love.

Susan stood still, staring at Freddie's contorted face, twisted with such ferocity that it was no longer recognizable. Love? Love *that*? If Freddie were herself, it would be easy to love her. But she was one of *them* now, and hate was the only possible—

To purify, you must love.

Slowly, reluctantly, Susan lowered the dagger. The blue light dimmed, the power and energy in her arms diminished. Her fingers numb, she dropped the dagger onto the floor. Without it she felt weak, vulnerable, powerless. Snarling, Freddie reached out with her foot and kicked it away. She

179

hunched over, ready to charge.

"Susan!" Angie screamed. "Pick up the dagger! Susan!"

Susan lifted her arms and put them around the hunched figure. "I love you, Freddie," she whispered.

Freddie's face twisted and she reeled, pulling away from Susan. There was a burst of yellow flame, a sudden scorched smell, and the candle went out as if it had been snuffed. The room was pitched into sudden and total blackness. Even the blue brilliance of the dagger had been extinguished. Outside, another squall rocked the building, and there was a loud, splintering crash.

"Susan?" Angie asked. Her voice rose hysterically. "Susan? Freddie? Are you all right?"

"I think so," Susan said limply. She felt as if she had suddenly been drained of all her life, just as the light had been drained from the dagger.

Freddie moaned.

There was the scratch of a match, and Angie relit the candle. Susan saw that Freddie was sitting in the middle of the floor, a dazed look on her white face. Her T-shirt was scorched across the shoulder. Her eyes looked almost normal again, though, and the red marks on her neck were beginning to fade.

"Will somebody please tell me," she said thickly, "what's going on?" She felt her jaw.

"Which one of you guys punched me out?"

Angie rushed over to her. "How do you feel, Freddie?"

Freddie made an impolite noise. "Lousy," she said. She struggled to her feet, leaning on Angie. "I feel like I've just gone three rounds with the current heavyweight champion."

Susan's legs felt rubbery. She sat down on the bed. "How much do you remember of the past few days?"

"Enough," Freddie said grimly. "So was I really a vampire? I mean, did I drink . . . *blood?*" she whispered in horror.

"No, you didn't," Angie hastened to reassure her. "Susan saved you before you were completely transformed."

Freddie looked at Susan. "Wow. Where'd you learn how to do that?"

"It's a long story, Fred," Susan said. "I don't think we've got time for it right now."

"Well, thanks anyway," Freddie said. "It was pretty awful while it lasted." There was a wry twist to her mouth. "I guess this means I've got to look for another singing job, huh?"

Susan managed a grin. "Next time check references first, huh?" She reached into her pocket and pulled out one of Aunt Carlota's silver crosses. "Here. This is for you. Wear it, and it will protect you."

Freddie looked at it. "I never thought of myself as the religious type," she said. "But after what I've been through—" She slipped it over her head.

"You'd better have these, too," Angie said, giving her a couple cloves of garlic.

Freddie wrinkled up her nose. "You've got to be kidding."

"I wish," Susan said grimly. She stood up. "Okay. Let's get going."

"Get going where?" Freddie asked, looking from one to the other. "I feel like I've been gone for the past week. I'm not going anywhere, except maybe back to bed for a couple of days. Anyway, haven't you heard? There's a hurricane happening out there."

"Forget the hurricane," Susan said. "And forget how you feel. We've got work to do." She picked the dagger off the floor and thrust it into her belt.

"What kind of work?" Freddie asked, confused. "You don't mean the Pizzeria, do you?"

"No, Freddie," Susan said gently. "There are others who need our help."

A look of sheer terror crossed Freddie's face. She held up both hands. "Wait a minute, you guys," she said, backing away from her friends. "We're not going *there*, are we? I can't. If I go to the Brothers' house, they'll get me again. They can, and they will."

"Juanita's there," Angie said starkly. "You don't have to go. But *I* do."

Freddie shut her eyes and stood silent for a minute. Then she blew out her breath and opened her eyes. "Well," she said, "I suppose it's only fair to hand in my resignation in person." She rubbed a hand through her red hair. "Too bad." She sighed. "It looked like a *very* steady job. Eternal, if you get what I mean."

Susan put her arm around Freddie's shoulders. "I'm sorry for the way things turned out," she said.

"Yeah, me too," Freddie replied. "But now I know what they mean when they talk about soul music."

Fifteen

~~~~~~~~~~~~~~~~~

Susan stopped her Honda in front of the cemetery, down the street from the Brothers' two-story Victorian, and turned off the ignition. It was early afternoon, but the blowing gray-green clouds cast an eerie, ominous twilight over the city. Gusting in off the Gulf, the wind filled the air with a fine salty mist and bent the palm trees like beach grass. Driving through the downtown area, Susan had seen that the streets were emptying fast, as people finished their storm preparations and headed for shelter away from the fury of the hurricane. With the sidewalks deserted, signs taken down, and windows boarded up, Galveston liked as if it were bracing for war.

That was how Susan felt, too. Braced for war.

It is your time to do battle, Aunt Carlota had said. Susan sighed wearily. The last struggle, with whatever evil power had filled Freddie, seemed to have taken all the strength out of her—and Freddie and Angie must feel even worse. None of them were ready to do battle with anybody, much less the darkest powers of the universe. She would far rather start the car again and go home to the everyday world of Mack and Betty and the boys. A world where vampires were something you laughed at in old TV sitcoms, and the hurricane would be the most powerful elemental force she would ever have to face. She would much rather go someplace quiet and think about Drew.

In the front seat next to Susan, Angie swallowed a sob. She was looking at the Brothers' house.

"Brad?" Susan asked softly.

Angie nodded. Her brown eyes were filled with tears. "He really thought he'd found a home here," she said bleakly. "He loved being a Brother. It gave him something to live for."

And something to die for, Susan thought to herself, *and to kill for*. But she couldn't say it out loud, so she just put a comforting hand on Angie's arm.

Angie brushed the tears from her eyes. "It's no use crying for Brad," she said fiercely, "when it's

186

Nita who needs us. Come on, let's go before the storm gets any worse." At that moment the wind ripped a large branch off a tree by the curb. It crashed to the pavement inches from the front of the car.

Freddie swallowed noisily. "Are you sure," she asked, "that this is the best thing to do? It's really blowing a gale. And what if we—I mean, what if the Brothers . . ." Her voice trailed away.

What if. Two words Susan didn't dare ask herself. "I guess there aren't any guarantees in the vampire extermination business," Susan said, trying to make a joke out of it. "But we're doing it anyway." She opened the door and got out.

Framed by shrubs and dark trees, the house loomed large on its narrow lot. Somebody had boarded up the big front window, and there were hurricane shutters over the other windows. Susan shivered. With the shutters closed the house looked like a huge gray mausoleum.

Bending into the lashing wind, they walked up the front sidewalk. Susan wasn't sure whether it was because she was extraordinarily sensitive now, after her encounters with the forces that had inhabited Freddie and Angie, or whether it was the house itself—but a feeling of chill foreboding seized her, and her stomach cramped.

"Do you think we ought to go around back?" Freddie whispered as they stood at the bottom of the porch steps. "Sort of sneak up on them?"

"No," Angie said firmly. "We have to go through the front door." She looked at Susan. "Do you have that bag of herbs Aunt Carlota gave us?"

Susan pulled the bag from her pocket and looked at it uncertainly. Aunt Carlota had said she should use it to purify the house, whatever that meant. But the bag felt nearly weightless in her hand. It contained less than an ounce of dried plants—not very potent medicine to cure the kind of evil the Brothers embodied. Suddenly there was a blast of wind that almost swept them away. Behind them they heard a sharp crack and a ripping noise, and the girls grabbed for one another and turned. The ancient pecan tree beside the walk was toppling over, as if it had been pushed by a giant hand. It lay now across the entire front yard, blocking the way to the street.

Freddie stared at it, white-faced. "I guess that means I can't go back and sit this one out in the car."

"Sit this one out?" Susan tried to laugh. "You'd miss all the action."

"Oh, yeah?" Freddie muttered. "Listen, this kind of action I can miss out on any day of the week. I'm basically chicken when it comes to blood."

Angie shuddered. "Do we have to talk about blood?"

"We have to talk about what we're going to do once we get in the house," Susan said.

"There's no time for talking," Angie said urgently. She grabbed Susan's hand and started up the steps. "Let's just do it."

"Even if we don't know what we're doing," Freddie said darkly, following them, "is anybody taking notes? This would make one heck of a made-for-TV movie."

The front door was open a crack. Inside was a chill, musty blackness, like the inside of a tomb. Angie pushed the door, and it gave a shrill creak.

Freddie jumped.

Not quite sure of what she was supposed to do, Susan opened the cloth bag and sprinkled the herbs on the threshold. As she looked down at the petals and dried leaves, they began to smoke. A clean, flowery fragrance filled the air, and the musty odor began to fade.

As the sweet-smelling smoke rose around her, Susan felt stronger and less afraid. Out on the street the winds seemed to have stopped, as if the herbs had some sort of magical power over the storm. It was almost as if time had frozen. She remembered that in the center of a hurricane was something called the eye, a space of intense quiet around which the winds swirled furiously at maximum force. She felt for a moment as if *she* were the eye of the storm, surrounded by forces that raged out of control, while within her was calmness and strength. Then, with a decisive gesture, she pulled the plastic dagger out of her belt and held it up.

In her hand the dagger glowed like a neon tube and illuminated the hallway. Behind her Angie pulled in her breath, and Freddie whistled softly.

The dagger was a beacon in the darkness, pulling them forward into the chill blackness of the house. Susan felt guided by some invisible power. It coursed through her, lending her a strength she didn't know she possessed. All her fear was gone now. She felt invincible, ready to confront any power, no matter how dark or how evil. And she didn't have to think about what to say or do. The words were there in her heart, on her lips.

She turned and struck the dagger hard against the doorjamb. "In the name of all that's good," she said loudly, "I command the evil to be gone from this place."

Everything happened at once. A searing flash struck the door in front and framed it in brilliant blue fire, so bright they couldn't look at it. The door itself went flying outward, and all the air in the house rushed through the opening in a screaming blast, nearly pulling the girls with it. In the front parlor the boarded-up front window exploded outward, sheets of plywood sailing like playing cards and shards of glass flying everywhere. With the blast came a heavy, putrid odor of something long dead, and the smoldering smell of something burning. From somewhere deep inside the house, Susan heard a shrill squeak, then another and another, a chorus of earsplitting screeches. Soon they were surrounded by a raspy cloud of dark, leathery wings, beating and scratching at them.

"Bats!" Angie screamed, and cowered against the wall, frantically shielding her head with her arms. For a long moment the hallway was filled with hundreds of the huge red-eyed creatures. Then they swirled out into the storm and vanished. The door swung shut behind them, leaving the girls standing in total darkness, with only the blue light of Susan's dagger to see by.

Freddie brushed the hair from her eyes. "Wow, what an *effect*," she whispered with a laugh that sounded like a rusty hinge.

"Is it safe to go on?" Angie asked.

"Go on?" Freddie said, alarmed. She peered ahead at the end of the hall, where the stairs rose into the blackness. "How do we know all the bats are gone?"

"We don't," Susan replied. "Not for sure. And we don't know that they were bats."

"What else could they have been?" Angie asked, shuddering.

Freddie stared at Susan. Her voice dropped to a whisper. "Are you saying they might have been—?" Her eyes lit up. "You mean we've driven them out? We've won?"

Angie shook her head grimly. "If those were vampires flying out the door, we haven't won, we've lost. They've *escaped*! They're free to go anywhere!"

Susan's mouth felt dry. The batlike creatures— were they the spirits of the Brothers' old groupies? Or the Brothers themselves, flying out into the storm to search for a new home, a new base of operations? She felt her heart begin to pound, the fear return. Or were the Brothers still in the house, hidden in its nooks and crannies, waiting for the storm to end, darkness to fall?

Angie's hand dropped. "We're not going to find Nita, standing here chattering," she said. She grabbed Freddie's hand and gave Susan a push. "Let's go."

Susan raised the dagger in front of her, and the three girls walked toward the end of the entrance hall. By the vivid blue light of the dagger, Susan could make out a stairway slanting steeply on the left. Beyond that, darkness. The house was filled with an oppressive silence that weighed down on them like a heavy blanket. The burning odor got stronger with each step.

Angie clutched her arm. "Look!" she gasped, pointing up the stairs. "It's Nita!"

A faint golden light appeared at the top of the stairs, and Juanita stood in its glow. She was wearing a gauzy white dress that drifted around her softly rounded figure. Her black hair was pulled back with a narrow white ribbon, and she was smiling dreamily, her lips a deep rich red against pearly teeth, her skin creamy, translucent.

Susan's eyes widened in surprise. She remembered Juanita as a plump, pretty girl who always made the most of her natural good looks. But this girl was beautiful. Strikingly, incredibly, *unnaturally* beautiful.

"Hello, Angela," Nita said softly. Her voice was warm and melodious, welcoming. She held out her hand.

"Oh, Nita," Angie breathed thankfully. "I'm so glad you're all right! I've been so worried about you." She beckoned. "Come on—let's go home before the storm gets any worse. Mom and Dad are going to be frantic."

Nita laughed, a delicious, silvery laugh. "There's no need to worry," she said. "We're safe from the storm here." She leaned forward. "Come on up, Angie, and bring Freddie and Susan with

193

you. We're having a hurricane party."

Angie put her foot on the stairs, but Susan pulled her back. "Something's wrong," she whispered. "I can feel it."

"But that's my sister," Angie said, pulling away from Susan. "I have to go to her."

"No," Susan said. The air had grown much colder, and there was a draft blowing down the stairs. Behind Nita, Susan could see a dark space, blacker even than the emptiness beyond the stairs.

Freddie frowned. "Susan's right, Angie. Nita looks too good to be true. Something strange is going on here."

At the top of the stairs Nita leaned forward. "Angela," she called in a singsong voice. "Please, Angela, come up. There's something I want to show you."

Angie wrenched her arm free. "I don't care what you guys say, I'm going up there. I'll get her and bring her down, and then we can all leave. The Brothers must have gone, anyway. Flown away with those . . . things."

The draft chilled the marrow of Susan's bones. "No," she whispered, reaching for Angie. "He's here. Flint's here. I know it."

But Angie wouldn't be held back. She was taking the stairs two at a time. At the top she threw her arms around Nita, who stood unmoving, still smiling her dreamy, unearthly smile.

"Oh, Juanita," Angie cried, "I'm so glad I found you." She put her arm around her sister's shoulders. "Come on, we're going home."

A looming black shadow stepped out of the darkness. A hand fell on Angie's shoulder. Angie gave a scream and clutched Nita. Susan tensed as the figure stepped forward, and her blood turned to ice. *Flint!*

A sudden blast of wind shook the house. Something hit the roof like a shower of stones. The bricks from the chimney, perhaps.

"The storm is worsening," Flint said in his accented English. "Surely you will remain with us for a small hurricane party." He chuckled dryly. "Even if our other guests have been forced, shall we say, to take rapid flight. What is it they say? We shall make beautiful music together."

Beside Susan, Freddie was staring upward, her face lit. "Flint!" she cried.

Flint turned, looking down at them. "Ah, Frederica, my love," he said in a velvety voice. "I am so glad that you have come, too. Without you our party would not be complete." He smiled warmly. "Come, my dear. Come and join your friends."

Susan put her hand on Freddie's arm. "Stay here, Freddie," she commanded. "I'll go up and bring Angie and Nita down."

But Freddie's eyes, dazed, were fixed on Flint. Moving like a sleepwalker, she took a step up the stairs.

"Freddie!" Susan cried. "Don't do it! Don't give in to him!"

Flint's laugh was like the grating scrape of a fingernail on a blackboard. "Ah, Susan. How refreshing your caution is. I must confess that your resistance intrigues me far more than your friend's too-easy responsiveness. You are strong, Susan, and powerful. What a joy it would be to join your power to my own. And what a marvelous gift our union could give to you, to immortalize that power you hold." His smile grew seductive and he paused, his dark eyes fixed on hers. "You would perhaps permit me to invite *you* to our little party, in Frederica's place?"

"Yes," Susan said boldly, meeting Flint's eyes. "I'm the one you want." She pushed Freddie aside and started up the stairs.

Freddie gave a desperate moan. Her knees buckled and she fell against the wall, stretching out her hand. "No, Flint! Not Susan," she cried. "*I* want to come! *I'm* the one who loves you, not her!"

Flint chuckled. "Your time will come, dear Frederica. For now you must wait there." He stepped in front of Angela and Nita. His voice was commanding. "Do you come to me of your own free will, Susan?"

"I do," Susan said. "I give my consent." Her heart was pounding, and her breath was coming in shallow gasps. The confidence, the invincibility she had felt when she struck the dagger against the door, was all gone. It had drained away, taking all her strength with it. But there was only one direction she could go—up. Into whatever horror awaited her there.

"Then come, my love," Flint said, and raised his hand. He smiled. "And bring your little toy, if it amuses you."

Her hand trembling, Susan raised the dagger. By now she was used to the sensation of energy surging through it as it began to pulse with blue fire. But she wasn't prepared for the enormous electrical jolt that nearly knocked her off her feet, nor for the blue light that enveloped her entire body. She remembered what Aunt Carlota had said about the storm concentrating the power. But if the force in the dagger was stronger, wouldn't Flint's power be stronger, too?

"Ah," Flint said, "a touch of theatrics. Is this the plaything that so unsettled our guests that they took wing and flew away?" He pulled himself up, looming over her at the top of the stairs, his eyes black and burning, his smile taunting. His voice was full of disdain, and Susan could see his long white teeth gleaming.

Susan didn't reply to his teasing question. She

put her right foot on the stairs, then her left, then her right, concentrating on taking one step at a time. Slowly she moved toward the blackness that was Flint. Somehow she had to get close enough to touch him with the dagger, and she could destroy him as she had Bishop.

But the thought of coming within arm's reach of that shadowy figure was almost paralyzing. If she was close enough to touch him, *he* could touch her, pull her against him, bare his teeth . . .

At the awful thought Susan's hand began to tremble so hard, she almost dropped the dagger. The blue light that had enveloped her began to fade, the power to seep away. Her knees and arms felt rubbery. Flint was right. It was only a toy, a plaything. How could she hope to destroy such unspeakable evil with a child's plastic dagger? As the doubt flooded through her, the blue light began to fade from the dagger itself, like the dying flame of a candle.

"You see?" Flint laughed. "You think to conquer me with a toy. If I were you, my dear, I would not press my luck." He raised his hand, beckoning her closer. "Come, Susan. I invite you. Drop the trinket—it means nothing. You see? It has lost its power."

Susan stopped still, almost at the top of the stairs. *I don't think I'd better press my luck.* It was Drew's line. At the thought of it she remembered Drew's fingers on her face, her question, *How did you get here?* And his answer, *Didn't you invite me?*

"Drew," she whispered urgently. "Drew, I invite you!"

Flint laughed. "He cannot help you now, my dear. You are mine."

Susan closed her eyes, trying to concentrate. Where was Drew? Was her power so weak she couldn't make him hear her? Or was Flint's power so strong that it drowned hers out? The moments stretched out endlessly as she waited for Drew to appear. Perhaps it was the energy of the storm that was keeping him away.

Behind her Freddie broke the silence with a whimper. "You see, Flint? She doesn't care about you. It's someone else she's inviting. She cares for another. *I'm* the one who cares about you, Flint."

Flint's laugh was hard, grating. "She will care."

Susan screwed her eyes shut and clenched her hands. "Drew!"

"Hey, you're doing fine," a conversational voice spoke at her shoulder. "Don't panic."

Susan turned. A shadowy form stood beside her. "But I'm so frightened."

"Of course you are," Flint said, sounding smug. "You should be frightened."

"He wants you to be afraid," Drew explained.

"He's counting on it. Fear drives out power." He chuckled. "But you don't have to be afraid of him. He can't take what you won't give him. Remember that."

"Susan," Flint commanded. "Give up the toy."

Angie stepped forward. "No, Susan!" she cried. "Don't give it up."

Susan held up the plastic dagger so Drew could see it. "The power's gone," she said. "The light's out."

"No, it isn't," Drew said calmly. He took Susan's hand and touched the tip of the dagger to her cheek. It began to glow blue again, and she could feel the pulse of its energy. "The power isn't in the dagger or the cross or the herbs. It's in you. That's what Aunt Carlota told you. All you have to do is believe in yourself."

Susan stared at him. "You heard what Aunt Carlota told us?"

His pale gray-green eyes were amused. "Ghosts get around. It's one of the privileges."

At the top of the stairs Flint was leaning forward, frowning. "Forget about Drew, Susan. Come to me, my dear."

"I do have the power," Susan said more to herself than to Drew, or even Flint. She squared her shoulders and summoned all her strength—*her* strength. She held up the dagger so Flint could see it. Then she opened her fingers and let it fall. Its light paled, then flickered for a moment, then went out. In the silence she could hear Angie's horrified gasp.

"What did you say?" Flint asked. "Speak to me, Susan."

Susan raised her voice. "I said, you're right, Flint. The toy has no power."

"Ah," Flint said, with a sigh of deep satisfaction. His eyes gleamed smoky red in the dimness. "Then you will join our party without further delay, will you not?"

Susan looked up at him, daring to meet his eyes. Her heart thumped in her chest. "I don't have any choice, do I?"

"No. You have no choice." Flint's voice deepened, took on a magnetic quality. "Come, my dear."

Susan forced her rubbery legs to advance one step; then another. Three more, and she would be within reach of him. Within *his* reach. At the thought she felt mortally afraid. Why hadn't she held on to the dagger? If she had kept it, she might have a better chance. But without it Flint might think she was powerless, vulnerable. Without it she might be able to catch him off guard.

Two more steps.

Flint laughed softly, expectantly. His eyes held hers. "So. You come to me at last, on my terms! You, the sweet, stubborn one. You, the powerful one."

One more step.

Flint rubbed his clawlike hands together. His face was dark, his eyes flashing red with triumph, his wolfish teeth gleaming. "We shall see who is stubborn now, shall we?"

And then Susan moved. Softly, swiftly, she stepped up to Flint and put her hand on his heart. As she did, she felt her arm throb, she saw it turn incandescent, saw her flesh become transparent, saw her very bones. She recalled Aunt Carlota's wisdom.

"Love," Susan said softly, "is the undoing of evil."

At the sound of the words, there came a flash of fire and the smell of scorched flesh. Flint screamed silently and spun away, gasping for breath. His hands clawed at his chest. Behind him Nita cried, a high, sobbing cry.

Susan reached for Flint's arm. As she touched him, there was another fiery flash, an explosion. A whirl of dark air, a howling tornado of evil, gathered itself and rushed past Susan, down the steps, and through the open door, to join the storm outside.

It was over.

Susan collapsed on the stairs, completely drained. The world spun around her, her mind was a gray fog. She was vaguely aware that Angie had pulled her sister down the stairs toward her. Nita was sobbing hysterically, calling Flint's name, and

Angie was shaking her shoulder, saying something in urgent Spanish. Somewhere downstairs Freddie was yelling. Suddenly Freddie's cry penetrated the fog.

"Fire! The house is on fire! We've got to get out!"

Sixteen

Susan found herself sitting on something hard. It was the low stone wall around the cemetery. She was soaked through, and the chill gale-force wind was lashing her shoulders, whipping her hair. She lifted her face and let the rain wash it clean. She didn't care that she was wet. Her three friends were beside her. They were safe. The Brothers were gone. That was all that mattered.

Freddie was shaking her. "Are you okay, Susan?"

"I . . . I think so," Susan said, feeling dizzy. She licked the rain off her lips. It tasted good.

"Boy, we got out of there just in the nick of time," Freddie said.

Susan shut her eyes. As if it had been a dream,

she remembered Nita crying, hysterical, and Angie talking excitedly. Each sister had taken her by an arm, lifted her up, and pulled her down the stairs and out the front door, with Freddie coming behind. For a moment Susan wondered what had happened to Drew. But of course nothing could happen to him, she reminded herself. He was a ghost. Nothing could hurt a ghost.

"Look!" Angie said excitedly, pointing across the street.

Susan looked. Heavy gray-black smoke poured out the front door and the blown-out front window of the Brothers' house. Along the side, furious flames licked up the wooden wall to the roof. Susan knew that in a moment the whole house would go up. Despite the coming storm, small knots of curious neighbors had gathered on the sidewalk in front of the burning house.

"We should call the fire department," Nita said.

"Somebody's already called them," Angie replied. "Here they come now." Susan could hear the wail of a siren heading their way.

A fire truck pulled up in front of the house. Firefighters dragged out their hoses while others raced with axes and extinguishers around to the back of the house. The onlookers moved back out of the way, and several went into their houses to escape the growing storm. One of the firefighters ran back to the truck and got on the radio to put out a second alarm. At that moment the wind sucked a sheet of orange-red flame through the broken window with a roar like a blast furnace. The whole front of the house was engulfed in flames.

"With this wind they'll never save the house," Freddie said, shaking her head. "In a way, I'm almost sorry to see it go. It was a really beautiful house, even if the owners were a little twisted."

Angie turned to Susan. "Did *you* do that?" she asked wonderingly. "I mean, when you lit up the doorway with that blue flame, was that what set the place on fire?"

Susan shook her head. "Your guess is as good as mine." She pushed her dripping hair out of her eyes.

"It was awesome," Freddie said. "You're like the bionic woman." She stared at Susan. "Hey, have you thought of doing stuff like that for a living? I'll bet those guys out in Hollywood would pay you a bundle."

Susan put her head down on her knees. She ought to feel triumphant, right? She had faced the darkest, most awful power in the universe, and had beaten it. Why didn't she feel as if she had achieved something?

It was a question she couldn't answer. Maybe because her victory was only temporary. Flint and the Brothers were gone; at least in the form she had known them, they were. But their power remained. They could create new forms, be it here or in a different place. What would happen then? Would there be another battle? Or, next time, would they win without opposition, without a fight?

Freddie nudged her. "Here comes a fireman," she said in a low voice. "What are we going to say to him?"

Susan looked up. A man in a yellow slicker and helmet was coming across the street. "Get Nita out of here," she told Angie urgently, handing her the car keys. "She's in no shape to answer any questions."

Angie grabbed Nita's arm. "Help me, Freddie."

Freddie took Juanita's other arm. "We'll wait in the car for you," she said to Susan. They walked off.

The fireman came up. "I'm Lieutenant Patterson," he said. "One of the bystanders here thinks you were in the house when the fire started. Is that true?"

"Yes, that's right," Susan said. "I came with my friend to pick up her sister. There was another girl with us. We were on our way out when we smelled the smoke."

The lieutenant scrutinized her face as if he were trying to decide whether she was hiding anything. "Were the residents at home?"

"No," Susan said. "They weren't there. And I don't know where they are now," she added truthfully, anticipating his next question.

"I'll need your name for my report," he said, taking out a notebook, "and the names of your friends." Across the street somebody shouted and waved, and he stuck the notebook back in his pocket. "Hang around for a few minutes, will you?" he said. "Looks like we're turning in another alarm." He turned and sprinted across the street.

Susan sat on the stone wall, shivering. The storm was worsening, and she knew she ought to call Mack and let him know she was safe. But a few more minutes wouldn't hurt. She sat quietly, watching the roaring mass of flames. The house, and everything it seemed to symbolize, was coming to an end. *The end?* she thought bitterly. *Is it really the end? Or is it only the end of the beginning?*

A few minutes later the second fire truck pulled up. Right behind it a white van rounded the corner and screeched to a halt directly in front of Susan. CHANNEL FIVE, KGTX-TV, was printed in big red letters on the side. Two men got out. One threw open the side door, swung a television camera onto his shoulder, and ran across the street, where he knelt down and started filming the blaze. The other man, obviously a reporter, walked toward Susan. He wore a green nylon windbreaker with the hood pulled up over his head.

"Hi," he said. He turned so that he had his back to the wind, and stuck his hands in the pockets of the windbreaker. "Looks like we got here a little late. Did you see what happened?"

"Sort of," Susan said guardedly. "I think it might have had something to do with the electricity. There was some blue fire around the front door, then a lot of smoke." It was the same story she planned to tell Lieutenant Patterson when he came back for his report. It was the truth—or part of it, anyway. She hoped it would stand up to scrutiny.

"Anybody live there?"

"Some rock musicians."

A squall rocked the truck. A power pole at the end of the street blew over with a crash, sending a shower of sparks into the dark.

The reporter looked apprehensive. "Maybe we should get out of this wind. You're soaking wet."

Susan stood up. "I'm waiting to make a report on the fire," she said. "Your first hurricane?"

"Yeah. We don't get weather like this up in Dallas. Up there all we get is tornadoes. And I've managed never to be on the scene when one of those babies came churning through."

Something inside her turned over. "You're from Dallas?"

"Yes," he said. "I came down here a couple of weeks ago, chasing a story for one of the Dallas stations. I decided to stay, and I was lucky enough to get a job filling in at KGTX."

Susan swallowed. The goose bumps that had risen on her arms had nothing to do with the rain and wind. "Welcome to Galveston," she managed at last. "I hope you'll like it here." She looked at him, but all she could see was the hood of his windbreaker. "What did you say your name was?"

He turned to face her. "I didn't say," he replied. "But I think I'm going to like it here." His pale gray-green eyes lingered on her face. "In fact, I'm *sure* of it."

"Drew?" she whispered incredulously.

The guy grinned. "Yeah. Hey, how did you know?"

Susan smiled back. "I think maybe I saw you on television," she said.

About the Author

Nicholas Adams has written many young adult thrillers. Among his more popular books are *I.O.U.* and the series *Horror High*. When he's not writing, Mr. Adams likes to watch scary movies and read horror novels.

■ HarperPaperbacks *By Mail*

Read all of L. J. Smith's spine-tingling thrillers.

The Secret Circle

This new series from the bestselling author of The Vampire Diaries tells the thrilling story of Cassie, who makes a startling discovery when she moves to New Salem: She is the last of a long line of witches. Now she must seize her power or lose it forever. . . .

THE VAMPIRE DIARIES
by L.J. Smith

The romantic, terrifying chronicle of a dark love triangle: two vampire brothers and the beautiful girl who's torn between them.

**Volume I: THE AWAKENING
Volume II: THE STRUGGLE
Volume III: THE FURY
Volume IV: THE REUNION**

Look for:
TEEN IDOL
by Kate Daniel

**Volume I: THE INITIATION
Volume II: THE CAPTIVE
Volume III: THE POWER**
